EMBRACE
ASHER

THE BLACKSTONE BROTHERS

Z.L. ARKADIE

Copyright © 2020 by Flaming Hearts Press LLC

All rights reserved.

No part of this book may be reproduced in any form or by any electronic or mechanical means, including information storage and retrieval systems, without written permission from the author, except for the use of brief quotations in a book review.

ISBN: 978-1-952101-10-6

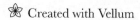 Created with Vellum

One

PENINA ROSS

Aunt Christine and I didn't get around to buying those sugary and fatty coffees since we were determined to find my mother. We had dodged such a devastating bullet with the corpse in the morgue not being Mary, and we heeded the warning from on high. We couldn't let my mom continue to remain missing. We needed to find her, and fast. I also desperately needed to find out who'd fathered me. So Aunt Christine drove us to the airport. After returning the rental car, she returned to Boston, and I was able to catch a four-thirty flight back to New Orleans.

As I waited for boarding, I tried to use my telephone to access the DNA company that had sent the results of my test. Unfortunately, I couldn't remember my password for their website, and when I tried to reset it, my phone ran out of power. I searched through my purse, trying to find my power adapter, but closed it after remembering that I had packed the adapter in my luggage, which I had checked.

I wanted to scream as I wrung my hands in anguish. It felt as if I couldn't buy a break, not even with a million bucks. Then boarding began, and that offered some relief as far as making me feel as if I was moving forward.

SOON I WAS SETTLED IN MY SEAT WHILE THE airplane climbed the sky. I focused on the trees and muddy plots of water below. Then, out of the blue, words that had been stuck in my brain for many years revisited me.

Know thyself. Always try to be aware of who you are. It's not going to be easy, but do it.

I finally remembered Christine had said that to me during one of our sit-downs when I was in medical school. Back then, I was ten times more exhausted than I was now. I was also perpetually depressed simply because of the demands of medical school. And missing my mother but not missing her at the same time compounded my misery. Those meals with my aunt were starting to reshape themselves in my mind. I was the one who was lethargic and barely present. She was empathetic to my state and allowed me to sit silently, be still, and just exist in her presence.

I hadn't realized how widely I was smiling until I turned and met the gaze of another passenger. It was a man, and he was handsome and clearly interested. I ripped my eyes away from his and stared aimlessly out the window. It was too soon to start another relationship. I still didn't know what was to come of Jake and me.

I wanted to throttle Jake because I disliked Gina so much. She hadn't had to be so cruel and cold. She'd made me feel as if I meant nothing to Jake and could never mean anything to him. Also, and I so hoped it wasn't true, we could be siblings. That thought made my heart feel as heavy as a boulder. Then I wondered whether the stranger's flirtatious ogling was a sign that I should look elsewhere for love.

No way.
Perhaps.
Maybe one day.

. . .

I DECIDED TO AVOID LOOKING OVER AT MY FELLOW traveler even when the flight attendant served my coffee and honey-roasted peanuts. Mostly, I continued gazing out the window, trying to figure out how in the world would I ever be able to put space between Jake and me? Gazing at his face felt as familiar as looking at myself in the mirror. It was as if I'd been acquainted with all his curves, lines, and pores my whole life. Were we soulmates? Or was our connection sparked by a blood connection? I clutched my belly as the possibility of the latter made me sick to my stomach.

WHEN THE AIRPLANE LANDED, I WAS STILL WIDE awake, and thinking about Jake. The next day, I would report for my shift. When or if I saw Jake, I would know whether he was my brother or not. It was our row's turn to exit, and the guy who'd been sneaking peeks at me all through the flight stood back to let me out before him.

"Thanks," I said, smiling tightly but avoiding eye contact. I didn't want to lead him on.

The guy continued giving me eye service in

baggage claim as we waited for our luggage to roll along the conveyer belt. I felt as if I was standing there wasting time. I certainly could've packed lighter and just carried a weekender bag onto the plane, but I'd been in such a panic after I spoke to Christine about my mother that I felt as if I were going to some faraway place where reality didn't exist. That was why I'd packed everything but the kitchen sink—and my computer, which I'd left at home by accident.

I had to admit it, though, I felt as if the whole world had been lifted off my shoulders, knowing my mom was still alive. I couldn't say for certain that she was, but Christine had said she was going to hire a private investigator to try to find her. I gave her permission to use all the funds that were sent to her from the trust that was set up to pay restitution for everything my mom had been through.

Then Jake came to mind. I didn't want to avoid him forever—maybe only a week or two. Then I wondered if I could continue engaging in sexual relations with my brother.

Hell no! My life wasn't *Game of Thrones*, which happened to be one of the few shows I used to watch with any semblance of regularity. Asher Blackstone being my brother would be a game changer. And the two of us perhaps being related almost made perfect sense. Maybe our electric, out-of-this-world, once-in-a-lifetime connection existed because we were family.

"Jeez," I groused as I almost missed my suitcase. I snatched it off the conveyer belt just in time not to have to chase it down.

"Do you need help with that?" the guy from our flight asked.

"She doesn't need help. I got it."

My body stiffened as my suitcase was carefully taken out of my hand. Then I turned around to see who the stranger was staring daggers at. "Jake?"

Or should I have said, "Asher"?

Two

PENINA ROSS

I almost refused to follow him to the car. First, I wasn't sure I was ready to see him yet. Second, seeing his face brought back my anger in spades. But regardless of my tumultuous emotions, we rode in the back seat of his spacious, chauffeured car. The glass separating the front from the back was rolled up as we headed toward the city.

"How was your flight?" Jake asked.

That question made a lot of thoughts shuffle through my mind, so I said the one that beat out the others. "How did you know I was flying in?"

He hesitated then readjusted in his seat. "I have my resources."

I quickly looked away from him. *Pen, don't look at*

his lips. Don't want to kiss him. I'd also noticed how far away from me he was sitting. Suddenly, I knew exactly what I had to do—I had to accept that fellowship in Boston. It was perfect timing. I'd never felt closer to my aunt. I wanted to continue nurturing a good and solid relationship with her. She could be the answer to my bouts with loneliness and hooking up with the wrong people to ease that feeling.

"What are you thinking?" Jake asked.

I wanted to turn and face him, but I didn't have enough willpower to stop myself from being dazzled by his pale and intense blue eyes. "What should I call you?" I turned and cleared my throat. "Asher or Jake?"

"Jake." He sounded sure about that.

"But your birth name is Asher Blackstone."

His eyebrows furrowed as his back seemed to hug the corner of the seat even tighter. I wasn't going crazy—Jake was indeed shifting himself farther away from me. Then I realized that he certainly didn't know about the possibility of us being siblings, so that wasn't the reason he was putting distance between us. In his many messages to me, he'd debunked Gina's claim that she was his girlfriend. Maybe they'd rekindled their bond while

I was away. If that was so, I would be heartbroken, but perhaps it would be for the best.

"What else are you thinking, Penina?" Jake asked again, reading my strained expression.

I heaved a sigh. "Jake, I have something to tell you that would probably throw a monkey wrench in all this relationship business between us."

His jaw flexed, and his eyes narrowed to slits. "Relationship business?"

"Well, you lied to me from day one, so ..."

"No, I didn't," he claimed. "I've confessed to you that I was hiding something. You allowed me to hold those secrets."

"But you said your secret wouldn't hurt me."

His eyebrows drew even closer together. "Gina is not my girlfriend. I hadn't seen her in six years."

I vigorously shook my head. "Not that." Suddenly, I felt the deep loss of Jake or Asher and what he could've meant to me for the rest of my life. "The thing is, you could be my brother."

"I know," he said, sighing.

My mouth fell open. "You do? How?"

He turned away to look out the window then glared at my face again.

"What?"

Jake reached into a pouch on the back of the

driver's seat. "Gina wrongfully went through your mail and opened this." He handed me an envelope.

I pressed my back against the seat before taking it. "It's my DNA results?"

"Yes." He almost looked sick saying that.

"It's not your fault that she opened my mail, Jake. So it's okay." My fingers were frantic as they took the contents out of the envelope. "But this was why I was in such a hurry to get home."

"The letter doesn't contain the information you're looking for," he said. Then he went on to explain that I would have to go onto the website, use a pin that was written on the page, and then use it to unlock instructions on what to do next.

"All of those steps?" I asked, feeling defeated by the process.

Jake nodded then cleared his throat. "I want to be with you when you make the call, if you don't mind."

"Sure," I said, reading the letter. It detailed all of what Jake had just explained to me.

We stared at each other in our usual way. I didn't know if I smiled first or if he did.

"Was the guy in baggage claim trying to pick you up?" he asked.

I shrugged, even though I knew the answer was

yes. There wasn't a single ounce of me that wanted to make Jake jealous. I also sensed that he was assessing whether I was considering looking elsewhere for companionship.

"The mystery still abounds," I said.

He nodded with certainty. "He was trying to pick you up."

"Well, in any case, I'm in no shape to start a new relationship."

"You're in a relationship with me."

We stared at each other again. Jake was still testing me. We both knew that being related would prevent us from moving forward as lovers. And I hated the fact that I wanted to do something like take his hand in mine or gently kiss his lips. However, it was apparent by how far we were sitting from each other that keeping our distance was the more responsible choice.

Jake coughed into his fist to clear his throat. "Why were you in Tampa anyway?" he asked.

I massaged the tension in my neck thinking about the last twenty hours. "The medical examiner's office in Tampa got in touch with my aunt and asked her to identify my mother's body." Thinking about it all made me weary again, so I sighed. "This morning, we learned that the dead woman wasn't my mom. But she had my mother's identification and a locket that belonged to her."

"Oh," he whispered with a nod. "Do you know where your mother is?"

I shook my head. "My aunt is going to hire a private investigator."

"I see," he said.

"I also learned my grandparents are still alive, but they're the very religious type who denounced and abandoned my mother and aunt, all because they didn't conform to their belief system." I was angry by the time I got to the end of that.

"You learned a lot on your short trip," he said.

"Yes." I looked deep into his eyes. "I also think it's best that I take that surgical fellowship in Boston."

His frown was so intense that he appeared as if he had just chugged a bottle of vinegar.

"That's your prerogative." His voice cracked as he readjusted in his seat. "Our hospital hasn't made you a counteroffer yet?"

I shook my head softly, already missing him so much. "I don't think they could if they wanted to. They don't have the budget."

"I see," he said, eyes narrowed to slits. Then he grunted thoughtfully.

JAKE KEPT TOUCHING ME, AND I WISHED HE WOULD stop. For instance, when the car pulled in front of my building, Jake rolled down the window separating the front from the back and told Kirk that he would let me out. He opened the door for me, and when we got out of the car, he gently put his hand on my waist as he slammed it shut. After he retrieved my suitcase from the trunk, we walked into the building, and he touched me on the waist again as he gave me space to enter first, then again before we stepped into the elevator. I didn't allow myself to think about all the making out we could've done on our way up to the third floor. I still longed for his touch, and it drove me crazy.

My residency ended in just over a month, so I wouldn't have to be around him much longer. However, I shouldn't have been so attracted to someone who could have been my long-lost brother. Thinking about how it felt sensual every time we kissed as well as all the mind-blowing sex we'd had was making me sick to my stomach.

But goodness gracious, he smells so good. And his stout cock that never fails to stimulate my hot spots … I'm going to miss his sexual skills.

"Do you have the key?" he asked as we reached the door to my apartment.

I jumped, startled. "Huh?"

"The key," he restated.

My skin felt flushed as I dug into the bottom of my purse while concluding Jake wasn't the only man in the world who knew how to give a girl a real intravaginal orgasm. Once I had the set in my hands, I absentmindedly held them out for him to take. "Here you go." I sounded winded.

Our fingers touched as he took them. My eyebrows fluttered as I skipped a breath. I hated that I showed him how his nearness made me feel. Thankfully, he didn't seem to notice as he turned away from me to stick the key into the lock. After he opened the door, he gave a lot of space for me to pass, and I appreciated his doing that.

I stopped in my tracks once I stepped inside. My apartment looked as if a tornado had hit it. My crap was everywhere, and I felt embarrassed that Jake saw my place looking like that.

"Excuse the mess," I said and started walking around, picking up plastic baggies that I packed my toiletries in, socks to wear on the airplane, and other knickknacks that I had cast aside after deciding to leave them at home.

Jake held up a hand. "It's okay. I've already been here."

I stood up straight as a board, picturing Jake in my messy bathroom and kitchen. "You have?"

He smirked. "I convinced Zara to let me in."

Jake went on to explain how he'd learned which airline I'd taken, and he had Kirk waiting in baggage claim for me to arrive until he was able to do it himself. His first surgery of the day had gone well, but he'd had to cancel the second one because before being put under, the patient confessed that she'd eaten a meal earlier that morning.

He and I laughed about that.

Jake crossed his arms and regarded me shrewdly. "So how do you feel about me entering your apartment without your permission?"

I rolled my eyes as I looked at my computer sitting on the desk. I pointed at it. "Did you try logging in?"

He raised an eyebrow. "I did."

I sniffed. "It's password protected."

Jake smirked. "I know."

We grinned at each other. If it were anyone else but Jake, I would probably have given him or her a lecture on privacy. But I still wanted him to know everything about me, just as I wanted to know everything about him.

"Well …" I nodded toward my computer. "I should go over there and figure out what you are to me."

His eyes smoldered, then he looked toward my bedroom. "That's an excellent idea."

Flustered, I unthinkingly tugged my loose topknot out of the band and forced my eyes not to stare at his package. I didn't want to see if he had a hard-on, not until I knew the results.

I FELT ECLIPSED BY JAKE'S PRESENCE AS HE STOOD behind me while I sat at my desk. That was his idea of giving me space I'd asked for. At first, he'd leaned over me, face beside mine. But I asked him to please move, and that was the new position he had taken, which was still too close for comfort.

I tapped my foot, waiting for my computer to finish booting. I was trying to think of something to say when my screen finally appeared.

"Oh, there it is," I announced.

He leaned over me again as I clicked on my browser and typed in the web address.

"Jake," I said, feeling giddy energy surge through me.

"Yes," he whispered, his mouth close to my ear.

"Really?"

"Really what?"

"I mean … You're very close."

He snorted a chuckle. "You know, we can figure this out either way," he said.

My fingers remained frozen on the keyboard. *What did he just say?* I was still processing his claim as I continued typing.

"Could you please, like, move away?" I sounded as strained as I felt.

"We're not attached in the family way, Penina," he said, holding his position.

"Our blood might be, though." I tapped the keys harder. "Give me space, please."

"You ever watched *Game of Thrones*?" he asked.

"Ha!" I scoffed as my computer finally coughed up the website. And he still hadn't backed away yet. "Yes, and do you remember how it ended for those maniacal and incestual twins?"

"I do. And in Jaime Lannister's defense, he wasn't maniacal. She was."

I chuckled as I clicked on the red button that read Results. "Well, the woman in our circumstances is never going to have sex with her brother."

Finally, he moved away from me to let out a belly laugh.

A box appeared, asking me to put in my pin number. I did it.

"What?" I yelped, looking at the big red banner telling me to call a number to hear the results and schedule an appointment with the local Spencer and Jada Blackstone Indemnity Fund coordinator that was assigned to my case. I was beyond frustrated. "This is just an unnecessarily complicated process."

"It seems Spencer's still all about control," he muttered.

"What?" I asked, obviously not because I didn't hear him. I wondered what he meant by that.

"Forget it. Listen, I want to take you somewhere," he said.

I felt my blank look intensify as I lost interest in whatever comment he made about Spencer. "Where?"

"Just trust me."

I pointed back at my computer. "Well, first I have to call this number."

"Don't worry about it," he said.

"I can't not worry about it. We have to know."

He pointed at my computer. "Not that way, though."

"Why not?"

"Again, trust me." He snapped his fingers. "Come on, babe, chop-chop."

I sighed. He'd called me babe, and that felt so intimate. I pondered whether I should insist that we keep our distance from each other until we knew for certain whether we were related by blood or not. With my luck, we were. However, whatever had made me gravitate to him from day one had taken full control of me. I was extremely curious about where he wanted to take me. Plus, my adventurous side was hard to put away once I'd been intrigued by something.

"I have no surgeries for the rest of the day, and you're off. We have no excuses. Let's go."

He held his hand out, which I reluctantly took. And, unfortunately, as soon as our skin touched, fireworks exploded inside me.

I quickly retracted my hand and shrugged, pretending I hadn't felt a thing. "Okay, then, lead the way."

Three

PENINA ROSS

t was a sticky and muggy late afternoon, but I had come to love the intense humidity that made ninety degrees feel like a sauna. I thought it was quite refreshing that we walked instead of easing into the back seat of Jake's hired car. It was better, actually. We shouldn't be in confined spaces at the moment. Anything could happen. For instance, my crazy brain was trying to persuade me to convince him to go somewhere with me where we could be alone, a place where no one else could find us, so that we could go at it like crazy before we learned the results. *What in the hell is wrong with me?*

"You're frowning," Jake said as we walked past Bernard's Bakery.

I blew out my cheeks as I sighed. "Well, I'm not happy about all of this." An idea struck me, and I pepped up. "Hey, we're both doctors. Let's get our blood tested." Then I groaned as I rolled my eyes, remembering the nosey lot who worked in the lab. "Forget it."

Jake chuckled. "I already thought of that."

"Who's Spencer?" I asked so quickly that I was positive I had cut him off.

"My brother."

"Then call him."

"We don't have to. The lab is running our DNA. I had Si do it."

I tried to rub the tension out of my temples. "Si? Si …" I repeated lowly. "Simon Brown. Chief Brown? You refer to him as Si?"

Suddenly, Jake took me by the waist and guided me to lean against the brick wall beneath an awning. As my head tilted back, our mouths nearly touched, and I could feel his warm breath ease into my mouth past my parted lips.

"You say you want to know more about me, then get ready, because there's a lot, and not much of it is good."

I swallowed. "I can handle it," I whispered.

As we stared into each other's eyes, those

passing by us didn't exist. The hums and roars of cars making their way up and down the street were mute. *Do we kiss? And if so, should it be deep, hard, and long?*

Jake was keeping his hard body away from mine. Rarely had I brushed up against him or felt him without him being at some stage of an erection. We were in the beginning stages of a fast-burning relationship and couldn't keep our hands off each other. Even during the moments when he lay beside me in bed, we rubbed, touched, and groped each other. And now we were forced to remain at a suitable distance from each other.

"I'll confess so this can pass," Jake said.

I gulped, hypnotized by the penetrating eye contact we held. "So what can pass?"

His fingers trailed down one side of my face until his thumb slid down the middle of my lower lip. "Soft … I want to kiss you."

I was overly sensitive to his touch as I croaked, "Me too." I cleared my throat. "We can't do anything about it except let it all pass. We're only human, Jake. It will—"

Without warning, his lips gently touched mine. The kiss wasn't lengthy or passionate, but it was still sensual, transmitting our love and longing for each other.

"There." He sighed with his eyes closed, as if he had to compose himself. A grunt that sounded deep in the back of his throat escaped him, then he tasted his bottom lip. "We should walk."

I nodded, only neither of us moved. The longer we stood there, the more anxious I became. I realized I had to take the lead when it came to breaking free from the strong magnetic current that linked us.

My head felt loopy as I walked. Jake was right by my side. We didn't hold hands, and we kept enough distance to appear like two people who had a casual connection walking on the sidewalk.

"So ..." I checked over both my shoulders. "You don't want me to refer to you as Asher?"

"No." His answer was firm.

"Not even in private?"

"No."

"You don't like the name?"

I studied his pinched expression as he glared ahead, and I recalled the comment he'd made during our first dinner together. He said he didn't like his name, and I'd thought he meant Jake Sparrow, but I was sure he was referring to Asher Blackstone.

I checked around us again. "But Jake Sparrow is a fake name?" I whispered.

"Not for long," he muttered.

"You're going to make it real?"

He sucked air sharply between his teeth. "Penina, so many questions, babe."

I raised a finger in objection. "No, Jake. You can't refer to me as babe."

He smirked. "I can always refer to you as babe. We're going to figure this out regardless of the results."

I scowled at the ground. That was the second time he'd claimed we were going to "figure it out." I didn't know about him, but I, for one, wasn't going to knowingly screw my brother, period. "Where are you taking me anyway?"

"It's on Dauphine," he said as we walked past parked cars and lots of people. We were in the touristy part of town, down on the lower edge of the French Quarter. I hadn't visited the area in a while. We kept moving away then back together while making space for other pedestrians to pass, so we didn't have to worry about maintaining a platonic distance. Shuffling past crowds of horny college students and drunken boys from every sort of fraternity under the sun, we conversed about some of the incidences from the past that Christine told me about but I couldn't remember.

"The brain has a way of self-protecting, doesn't it?" he said then trotted ahead of me to open the door of a bookstore.

"Yes, it does, but——" I raised my eyebrows and held them high. "You wanted to show me books?"

He pointed his head toward the inside of the shop, signaling for me to enter. "Only one book."

I narrowed my eyes playfully at him as I walked inside. Jake smirked and winked back. I beat back the desire to kiss him and breathed in the overpowering scent of old, printed paper. The place was far from a super-modern Barnes & Noble type of bookstore. Most of the books on the shelves looked worn. Large boxes that contained used books arranged by genres sat open for us to pick through if we were in the mood to hunt for something worth reading. Back when I was in college, before the semester started, I used to call at least a hundred bookstores like the one we were in, asking if they sold any of the text-books that were on my syllabus. Whenever I struck gold, I ended up buying a book that cost over hundred dollars brand new for only ten to twenty bucks.

I followed Jake along the stacks. "It seems as if you know where you're going," I said, sliding my finger across the spines as we passed.

Jake turned sideways but not all the way around. "I do know where I'm going."

"So there's something you want to tell me through a book, eh?"

He snorted a chuckle. "It can better explain where I come from than I can."

"How's that?"

"It's a lot of what we were just talking about," he said, taking care to keep his voice low. "When you're in it or involved, you can't see it unless there's someone on the outside looking in."

I nodded. "True."

At the end of the aisle, he turned the corner, and three girls who had just caught sight of him nearly lost their minds, keeping their dazzled gazes pasted on his magnificent face. I was glad when we turned another corner. The eager girls were annoying me. Then Jake stopped in the center of the aisle, and without having to search, he plucked a book off the shelf and held it out for me to take.

"This is for you," he said.

I hesitated, eyeing him suspiciously as I read the cover. "*The Dark Blackstones?*" I asked as I took it.

"It's about my family. If you want to know why I'm Jake Sparrow? Read this."

Once again, I noticed how close he was. I couldn't take a step back, or I would crash into the shelf, so instead I held up the book, putting it between us to create some distance, then read the cover.

"Written by Holly Henderson—that's a name with killer alliteration."

"She's my sister-in-law," he said without chuckling at my attempt to lighten the mood.

"Is this an unauthorized biography?" I asked.

Jake stepped closer. The book was against his chest, and I could feel the heat coming off his body. "She was invited to our estate for the Christmas holiday six years ago. I knew what my sister had planned, but I didn't approve. I …"

I waited for him to finish, but then I turned to see what he was watching. The three women who'd given him eye service earlier were in the aisle, pretending to be looking for a book.

"Come on. I'll pay for that," he said, nodding toward the opposite end from where they stood browsing.

When we made it up front, the cashier, an older gentleman who wore bifocals that were too big for his classically handsome face, couldn't stop staring and grinning at Jake either. Jake must've also noticed that the man was tuned in to him, because he seemed fidgety. After paying with a fifty-dollar bill, he told the guy to keep the thirty-eight dollars in change.

"You look familiar," the cashier said, remaining intensely focused on Jake's face.

Jake glanced at me.

"Aren't you related to one of those Blackstones?" he asked.

Jake smiled nervously. "Nope. But I get that a lot. That's why we're buying the book."

The guy grunted thoughtfully, unable to take his eyes off Jake. Then he shook his finger at him. "You're the triplet. The one that's been missing. Someone said they'd seen you in the area. And I've seen you in here before."

I worked like hell to keep my jaw from dropping, although I was sure my face had turned red. *A triplet?*

He was still pointing as he said, "They're accusing you of killing your father, and that's why you've been missing."

The cashier was reading all of Jake's reactions. For the most part, Jake kept his cool. He was no longer grinning and using charm to throw the man off, though. His face was expressionless. But the fact that he hadn't moved an inch was evidence that he was petrified.

The guy handed Jake his change anyway, and he automatically took it and stuffed into his pants pocket.

The cashier flashed a toothy grin. "Don't worry, though. New Orleans ain't concerned about what happens outside of New Orleans."

Without saying a word or looking at me, Jake turned and walked out of the store, leaving me standing there. I'd never seen him that flustered before. Even when the woman outed him three nights ago, he'd kept his cool. I had no idea what to do as I looked from the exit to the cashier. I felt as if I had to beg him to please keep his word and never mention that he'd seen Jake or Asher Blackstone around. I was afraid that now that someone in the general public had recognized him, Jake would run, and I would never see him again.

"Um …" I said.

The guy smiled weakly and went back to doing whatever work he had been doing before we came to the register. It was the weirdest thing. It was as if he'd said what he wanted to say, and since Jake was gone, Jake was now the furthest thing from the man's mind.

"Have a nice day," I finally said to the cashier.

"You, too, darling," the man said as if I were just any old customer he was being nice to.

Four

PENINA ROSS

At first, I thought Jake had left me behind, and quite frankly, I would've been okay if he had. He needed time to process what had just happened. And perhaps that jarring experience injected him with common sense. *Get away from your possible sister, whom you're attracted to. Get far away.* But as I walked back the way we'd come, I heard him call my name from behind. When I turned, he was standing right there.

"Are you okay?" I asked as he closed the gap between us.

"No. What the hell was that?" he asked with an uncomfortable laugh.

I shook my head. "I've never seen you that rattled."

He seemed unable to look me in the eyes when he shrugged.

"And you're a triplet?"

He scratched the back of his head. "I don't want to talk about it, Penina. It's in the book."

I glanced down at the title in my hand, respecting the fact that it contained all the answers I needed. "Well, what are you going to do now that you've been recognized?"

He checked over his shoulder then up the street. His energy felt erratic. After narrowing his eyes at whatever he had spied, he pointed his chin in that direction. "Look at where the crowd's going. There's a music festival. You want to go?" He was smiling again.

I shook my head as I jerked it back. "Are you serious, Jake?"

His sexy smirk was back and more seductive than ever. "I'm very serious."

"But …" I moved closer to him. "He just said you murdered your father," I whispered.

Jake's smirk faded as he garnered steady eye contact with me. "The man in the bookstore doesn't know what he's talking about. My father was on his deathbed for many months before he died. It was kept secret, which is why people have come up with their harebrained theories of how he passed. I did not kill my father. He was sick, and he died."

I didn't know what to believe when it came to Jake anymore. However, I had to go with my gut, and it told me that I should believe he was telling me the truth until I learned different.

I heaved a sigh, letting what had just happened in the bookstore drop. "You want to go to a music festival together?"

"I'm not asking anyone else to go with me," he said.

I nibbled anxiously on my bottom lip.

"We can eat, dance, have some fun …" he said.

I squished one side of my face. "Are you sure?"

"Penina, if the nature of our relationship has to change, then we'd better work on being friends only. Don't you think?"

I turned to watch a horse and buggy carting tourists gallop by. It sounded as if he was certain we were family.

"Did you give me the book because you know for certain we're related?" I asked, staring at the cover.

Jake took the book out of my hands and put it into my purse. "Out of sight, out of mind." He winked. "And the answer to your question is, I don't have the test results. Therefore, I can't confirm that you're not Randolph's daughter. However, I just have a hunch you're not."

I folded my arms. "Why not?"

"Because …" he started then stopped.

"Because?"

He shifted to stand closer. To those passing by, we appeared as if we were two people on the verge of kissing.

"Here's what you won't discover by reading the book," he said. "And remember what I said about my grandparents." He flicked his eyebrows up twice.

I jerked my head back as if his words had physically shocked me. "What are you insinuating? You and I both know the dangers of first-degree incest, like severe birth defects, schizophrenia, blindness …"

Jake held up a hand to stop me. "I was joking, Penina."

I shook my head emphatically. "Well, I'm not joking, Jake, or whatever your name is." I wasn't going to say Asher out loud, especially after the bookshop clerk knew who he was. "We had sex," I whispered. "We screwed, and now we're screwed."

After a long pause, Jake took a deep breath.

"Let's just have a good time. We'll wait for the results. And we'll figure out our next steps."

I crossed my arms, shaking my head continuously. It was as if he didn't get the gravity of what was happening between us. "You know, you alluded to the fact that we'll figure it out three times already. What the hell does that even mean?"

Jake rubbed the back of his head again. "I don't know, Penina. You're beautiful, that's for certain." He swallowed, and his gaze seemed to swallow my face appreciatively. "You don't look anything like my father, though I'm very certain you're Valentine's daughter, and I'm sorry about that, because he's still alive. He's in prison, thanks to my brother, but he's still alive."

My eyes grew wide. "In prison?"

"Yes. He was my father's accomplice."

"Accomplice in what?"

"It's in the book."

Frowning, I glanced down at my purse. "And I look like this guy?"

"His daughter, Julia."

My mouth was caught open. I blinked hard, and my eyes got stuck closed. "Daughter?"

"Penina …" He said my name so beautifully. "I've been waiting to make love to you because I know you need confirmation that we're not related. I already figured it out, so if you're not going to let me kiss you or take you to bed, then please, let's go have some fun."

IT WAS WHEN JAKE AND I DANCED TO THE SECOND song the band played that I realized we were out in public together and not that far from the hospital. Anyone who knew us could see us together, though I hadn't spotted anyone I knew, and when Jake dipped me and brought me up, narrowly avoiding tonguing me passionately, I understood why he felt it was safe enough for us to enjoy the festival. Most people who worked at the hospital would avoid a touristy event on a Friday afternoon.

Jake was a great dancer, though. He was naturally smooth, very much aware of how his body bent, curved, and gyrated to the musical notes. It was sexy how he moved his hips. I was hoping to God we weren't related, especially since his cock was hard each time he rubbed it against me. Apparently, he was sure we had no blood ties. If only I could take his supposition and run with it.

Then I remembered something and grabbed

him by the shoulders. "Jake, tonight's Courtney's party!" I shouted above the music. That was another reason hardly anyone from the hospital would be at the music festival, especially those from our ward. They were all getting ready for the highly anticipated soiree of the summer.

Jake slapped himself on the forehead then took me by the hand, leading me through the crowd. When we made it through the gate and were walking quickly along the river, he drew me close. Without a word, his tongue was in my mouth. As our lips pushed against each other with fire and desire, I decided he was right. My father was a monstrous man locked up in prison for being Jake's father's partner in crime, which in turn made him a letch. Our tongues whirled around each other without restraint. My head climbed toward the darkening sky. His mouth tasted so good. With each stroke of the tongue, I found it harder to stop kissing him. We were winded and not at all concerned about who was watching us as his mouth broke from mine. Then we pressed our foreheads together.

"So … I imagine you don't want to go public until we have the results," he said.

After that kiss, it was as if all my raw lust and

yearning for Jake had risen to the surface. If I spoke, I would mug his mouth with another deep kiss. If I didn't get control of myself, I would suggest we skip the party, head back to his penthouse without a moment to spare, and bang like rabbits, bears, and lions.

"When will you get them?" I asked breathlessly.

"Soon," he whispered. "Si put a rush on the results."

I immediately pictured everyone who worked in the lab. They were all headstrong. They hated rush lab orders. God forbid they worked beyond the scope of the normal protocol.

Jake smirked. "You rolled your eyes. Were you aware of that?"

I shifted my gaze away from his face to think about it. "No, I wasn't aware."

"There are lots of small habits I've noticed about you, and rolling your eyes is one of them."

"You're crazy," I said, smiling from ear to ear. It felt good to know someone was truly seeking to notice my patterns. It made me feel wanted.

I wanted to put my hands together and pray to the Almighty not to let us be siblings. It would be the worst joke fate had ever played on me.

WE STOPPED BY CAFÉ DU MONDE SO THAT JAKE could buy me beignets. The line reminded me of lines for a ride at an amusement park. However, Jake asked me to wait while he went to the kitchen. He said he knew a guy. No wonder the locals had figured him out. It was difficult to hide out in a place like New Orleans. The town constantly called its residents out to play. And it seemed that between the guy in the bookstore recognizing him and knowing a guy at one of the most popular spots on Decatur Street, Jake, who was obviously adventurous, had been out exploring the town.

Jake returned to me with two bags, each holding two hot beignets heavily dusted with powdered sugar. We strolled back to my apartment, eating and talking.

"Why don't you drive your own car?" I asked.

"Because I hate driving."

"Do you know how to drive?" I bit into the warm pastry and chewed, watching him curiously.

His eyebrows flicked upward. "What do you think?"

I tilted my head. "Was that a flirt?"

Suddenly, his cell phone chimed, and he winked as he answered it.

"Yeah, Si," he said then listened.

Whatever Chief Brown said next made Jake squeeze my shoulder. All the color had drained from his face.

"The results?" I mouthed.

Jake shook his head, answering me, then said, "I'll be right there."

Just as Jake was beginning to learn my quirks, I was starting to know his. He was definitely rattled and trying to hide it, especially when I asked if everything was okay.

"Someone needs a consult," he said.

He tried to convince me to let Kirk take me from my apartment, where I would collect my things, to the penthouse to get dressed. I let Jake know I didn't want to add all of those extra steps to my evening. I would rather walk back to my place, shower, and take a cab to Courtney's party. I was surprised he gave me no pushback. Instead, he kissed me on the forehead and said that he would see me later.

I was alone in my place and not stressing over needing to know if my mother was alive or why Jake seemed so anxious when he walked away from me. I flopped down on the foot of my bed then lay back. I wasn't that enthusiastic about getting ready for Courtney's party, either. A time existed when I would've done anything to be there, but all I wanted to do now was close my eyes, go to sleep, wake up in the morning, start rounds, and at some point the next day, learn about the test results.

"Or …" I said. I looked around for my purse, but then my phone played the chime that let me know that I had missed a call. The sound came from outside of my bedroom, so I got up and shuffled to the living room and retrieved my device from my desk. *I left it earlier.* I listened to the voice message from Jake, who said he would see me later at the party, was counting on me being there, and that I should not choose going to bed over attending. I tossed my head back and laughed. *How did he know I would grapple with going to sleep over interacting with Court and Rich?* Then he sent me a text message that read *And don't go anywhere near Greg Carroll.*

I blurted a laugh and texted back, *Don't worry, brother. No more professional athletes for me.*

I STARED AT THE SCREEN OF MY PHONE, WAITING FOR his reply.

. . .

I'M NOT YOUR BROTHER, AND I CAN'T WAIT TO SHOW you. And you'd better believe no more athletes. Only one neurosurgeon from here on out.

I SHOOK MY HEAD.

YOU HAVE LOADS OF CONFIDENCE, BROTHER, I TYPED and sent.

I'M RIGHT. DON'T WORRY. PENINA, I THINK I LOVE you, he wrote.

I STARED AT HIS TEXT WITH BULGING EYES. I HAD NO idea how to respond. It would be easier to say it back if I knew definitively that he wasn't my brother. I pressed my lips into a hard line. Whether he was a brother or lover, I knew one thing for certain.

I think I will always love you, no matter what, I replied.

. . .

HE RESPONDED RIGHT AWAY WITH A THUMBS-UP AND *Heading in. Save me a seat beside you.*

OKAY, I WROTE.

THEN HE SENT ME ANOTHER THUMBS-UP.

I STOOD VERY STILL WITH THE PHONE IN MY HANDS, hoping, praying, and praying some more that Jake was right. I looked like that Julia Valentine person. Then it dawned on me that the woman might be my sister. Only I was the result of a monstrous act committed by her father toward my mother.

A sick feeling began to spark in the pit of my stomach. I was beginning to wonder if I could truly have a good time at the party with all that was still up in the air. *But Jake said he'd be there.* I certainly didn't want him showing up at the party with me at home and leaving him as fresh meat for all the groupies that swarmed Rich and his friends like ants on candy. That was when I got a new burst of energy and traipsed to the bathroom to shower.

I HAD ON A ROYAL BLUE A-LINE DRESS THAT MADE my cleavage look like two succulent apples. Rich used to go crazy with lust whenever I wore the dress. Once, he sucked my tits all night and was so turned on by gorging on breasts that he actually came. Not only was that the power of that particular dress, but it was also the closest he'd ever come to doing me in the raw.

Of course, I wasn't wearing the dress for Rich. I'd put it on for Jake. For a moment, I thought it would be sort of cruel to seduce him, but then, at a party like the one I was attending, I had to bring my A game or shrink amongst all the tits, ass, and camel toe that the groupies were willing to put out there for Jake to salivate over.

I hated that I was suddenly worrying about insecure and vain stuff like that.

I applied more dramatic makeup than normal and took time to curl my long hair. All of my layers had grown out, which meant as soon as I had the time, I would make an appointment at Barbara's

Beauty Salon, which was across the street from my building, to get them back. Before leaving, I went to my calendar to make a note that I should check my schedule and contact Barbara for an appointment.

The letter from the DNA company captured my attention. I wondered why Jake hadn't wanted me to simply follow the instructions and make the call. I almost thought it had something to do with not giving his brother control. I sensed some sibling rivalry. Then I remembered him mentioning that his ex-girlfriend was in love with his brother. Perhaps that was it. Maybe that was why he'd run away from his ultra-rich family.

I liked Jake an awful lot and loved him too, but I would not let that get in the way of doing what was best for myself. The letter said that the line was open twenty-four hours a day. So I cast all of my trepidation to the wind and dialed the number.

I could feel my insides shudder as I waited for someone to pick up the phone. I went rigid when the ringing stopped and a voice came on the line.

"You have been identified as having a first-degree DNA connection with subjects of a special fund set up for victims and the family members of victims who have suffered sexual assault by one Randolph Blackstone and/or Arthur Valentine. A restitution fund has been set up on your and many others' behalf. At the sound of the beep, please speak your identification number and verify your phone number, and we will be able to release your parentage results once your credentials are verified and entered into our system. This will take between twenty-four and forty-eight hours. Also, be aware that you have the right to decline monetary or any sort of restitution paid from this fund, but we encourage you to accept compensation. And finally, your indemnity fund agent will send you an email to schedule your initial call. Thank you for taking the time to call us."

Then came the beep that officially ended the recording.

I struggled with whether or not I should speak my number. The prerecorded voice told me where I could find the number on my letter and to speak it then press pound when I was finished.

Finally, I thought, *What the hell.*

I said, "One-five-three-three-six-zero," then I pressed the pound key and left my phone number. The recorded voice thanked me and informed me that I could end the call.

Five

PENINA ROSS

There was a knock on my door as I raced around the condo, looking for my keys and wallet. I couldn't find either in my purse. As usual, I was a basket case.

"Who is it?" I shouted, searching my purse again.

"It's me, Kit Kat," Zara sang.

"Reese's Pieces!" I exclaimed as my hand landed on my keys.

I shuffled to the door and opened it.

We hugged, then I stood back to get a complete picture of her. She was wearing a strappy and slinky black cocktail dress, which made her three times as much the ravishing beauty as she already was.

"You look positively gorgeous," I said.

"No, but look at you," she said. "And I mean in every way. You know I was the one who let Dr. Sparrow into your apartment," she said.

I recognized her tone. Zara was about to pry. "I know," I said as I spotted my wallet on the sofa, wondering when the hell I had put it there. Then I thought that it might have fallen out of my purse when I tossed it onto the sofa earlier when Jake was with me.

"What's really going on between the two of you?" she asked.

I bit my bottom lip, fighting the urge to blurt our relationship from the beginning to the end, along with the fact that Jake might be a first-degree blood relative of mine, and that despite that, my body yearned for his touch.

"But don't say anything yet," she said, checking her watch. "Let's share a cab and get our asses over to Court's. We're already late." Then Zara raised her eyebrows twice quickly. "Unless you already have a date."

I caught myself at the beginning of rolling my eyes. Damn it, Jake was right. If he hadn't brought it to my attention, I would never have noticed myself doing it.

"Nope, Jake's in surgery."

Zara leaned back, stretching the corners of her mouth downward. "Jake, huh?"

I could feel an intense frown scrunching my face.

"Wait, then it's no more Jake?" she asked.

"Wait," I said throwing my hands up next to my ears.

"What?" She sounded worried.

"Deodorant. How the hell could I forget to put deodorant on?" I raced to the bathroom.

"You see, I no longer find myself in the state that you're in," Zara said as I rolled the deodorant stick under both my armpits.

"Lucky you," I called as I added a dot of my expensive perfume while I was at it. I had no idea what brand it was. The salesgirl had told me it was popular and smelled divine. I tried it, and she was right. It had a delicious scent as long as I didn't overdo it. So I added a gentle dot to the other side of my neck.

Zara shouted, "Come on Pen, jeez."

I took one more look in the mirror and gave myself a thumbs-up. *Jake is going to love my tits in this dress.*

"Here I come."

EVEN THOUGH WE WORE HEELS, ZARA AND I DID A fantastic job of power walking to the elevator. As we got in, I knew she couldn't wait to question me profusely about Jake. Pretty soon, I was going to feel as though I were a witness on the stand, being asked all sorts of objection-worthy questions by the prosecutor. That was why I decided to bombard her with questions before she could start with me.

"So how's your boyfriend?" I asked her.

"What boyfriend?" Her tone was lackluster.

"The one you were with when we last spoke. He was in the shower, and you were whispering, saying that you were in love with him."

She scrunched her face. "I said that?"

"Yes, you did. I guess it's no longer the case?"

The elevator doors opened.

"It's still the case," she said, eyes to the floor, as she walked out. "Well, it's almost the case." Then she groaned. "Maybe not."

Something was very wrong with Zara. I was on the verge of taking her by the shoulders, something we did when we wanted to get each other's full attention, but as soon as we stepped out into the warm night, I was stopped by the sight of a black limousine. The back door was already opened, and Kirk, the driver, was smiling pleasantly with his gaze bouncing between Zara and me.

"Dr. Sparrow would like to make sure you arrive safely at your destination. May I take you there?" he asked.

In many cases, I never knew what sort of eye candy a man was until one of my girlfriends stared at him as if he were a lollipop. Zara's gaze constantly flitted over to Kirk, and his did the same, as he often stole looks at her through the rearview mirror. The energy flowing between them was strong, and I almost felt like a third wheel.

The limo was the same one Jake and I had ridden in to the masquerade party. It had a full bar next to the door, stocked mostly with chilled bottled water, but this time there were chocolate-covered strawberries, pralines, and turtles sitting next to a fresh bouquet of roses.

Grinning from ear to ear, I read the card.

"What does it say?" Zara asked.

I stuffed it back in the envelope. "It's private." It read *I can't wait to be inside you.*

She grunted thoughtfully. "A neurosurgeon with his own personal driver?" Zara said, reaching for a strawberry. "And it's so unnecessary in New Orleans, which means he's pretty loaded. Only the filthy rich spend this much money on frivolous crap." She bit into the strawberry. "Oh, that's good."

Kirk snorted a chuckle, which was even more evidence that he was sweet on Zara. Jake was his employer, and she had just criticized him. The beautiful Zara had stolen his loyalties away from Jake.

"Jake is a strange individual," I said to pacify her.

"Oh, okay … You're not engaging, then? Is that it?"

I shrugged. "Engaging in what?"

"His money. How rich is he?"

Zara and I stared at each other until she began laughing.

"You're so damn good at keeping secrets. I mean, not one person knew I was in DC, only you and Angela, who can keep a secret almost as good as you can." She polished off the strawberry.

I shifted abruptly in my seat, signaling a

welcome change of subject. "Speaking of DC, when are you moving there?"

Kirk was watching her again. Zara looked down at her lap and shrugged.

"What does"—I mimicked her shrug—"mean?"

She looked at me. "What does what mean?"

I showed her the shrug I'd copied from her.

"I don't know, Pen. Maybe I was too hasty when I left."

I glanced at Kirk. I didn't want to mention the other guy as long as they had chemistry flowing between them. But I so very much wanted to know what had happened with that relationship.

"Then you're ready to be a surgeon again?" I asked.

Zara groaned as she sighed. "I wouldn't go that far."

"But Zara, you've almost completed the program."

She threw her hands up. "Pen! Because you're almost done with something doesn't mean you have to finish it. Especially if you don't love it, and I hate it."

My frown gave me a slight headache. To say I was confused was an understatement. "Then what in the hell were you hasty about?"

"Leaving New Orleans?"

"And not quitting your neuro residency?"

"Hell, no. I'm done with that."

For some reason, the feeling of being stuck in intense crisis mode gripped me. "But it doesn't make any sense, Zara," I said, flinging my hands emphatically. "You were almost at the finish line."

"You said that already."

"Well, I'm saying it again. It's right there in front of us, and we're about to cross it. So why are you quitting now after thousands of dollars and hours spent becoming a surgeon? And you're a damn good one at that. Why now?"

Zara slumped as she sighed. It was as if she'd blown all the tension out of her body. "You're right about the thousands of hours and dollars. Sure, I put the time and effort into being a surgeon, but I didn't do it for me. It's over. I'm an adult. I'm not a traditionalist like my parents are, and therefore I'm not interested in pleasing them anymore. So as far as I'm concerned, the bill is on them, not me." She took her phone out of her tiny purse. "I want to show you something."

I was still processing her reason for leaving the program. She'd said that she was only a surgeon to please her parents so many times I couldn't count. I'd never taken her seriously because she was one of the best in our program. Not only that, but I could never connect to her circumstances. I'd never had parents tell me I couldn't do this or that, parents who thought I belonged to them and not myself. The dark circles under Zara's eyes were gone. The dusty-rose red was in her cheeks. Her appearance was healthy, almost angelic. From the outside, leaving the program seemed to have done her some good.

However, I just had one more thing to say. "But how did you stick around so long? Usually, those who are in it to parent-please, they screw up early and often. You never did that."

She shuffled through photos. "Because I take pride in everything I do," she said matter-of-factly as she stopped on a photo of a woman wearing a long silver gown and hunching her shoulders. The picture looked as if it had come out of the pages of a fashion magazine.

I was about to ask why she was showing it to me when she said, "I'm the photographer. I've been hired by *Fashion F Mag*. They're one of the hugest publications in the business. Not only that, but they've started dabbling in e-commerce as well, which means they're going to be around for a while."

Her eyes danced excitedly as she spoke about how she was able to split her time between New Orleans and New York.

"How the hell did this happen? I thought you were interested in politics," I said.

Finally, Zara rolled her eyes and rubbed my back. "Pen, it's all right. I'm going to be fine."

I pressed my lips together, wondering why she'd said that. Perhaps I was more perturbed by her life decisions than necessary. It wasn't healthy on my part.

"You can't control the things in your life that you love, Pen, and that includes me. I'm happy you're upset, because again, that means you love me like a sister. And I love you that way too. Seven years, we've been each other's family. You know, the kind we pick, not the sort we're stuck with." She shook her head. "Can't you see that you're the reason I stayed? You're my family."

My sinuses became tight as Zara and I stared at each other. Suddenly, I realized why I was taking her leaving so hard. We had spent more time together in the past seven years than I had with anyone in my life. It hadn't felt as if we were two peas in a pod until that very moment. Since day one as interns, she and I had melded. We'd assisted each other in every assignment, examination, and surgery, and had sometimes forsaken sleep for twenty-four hours, trying to figure out how to irrigate a difficult brain bleed without damaging surrounding nerves. Then we had lunch or dinner, and Zara talked about anything but what was going on inside the hospital. Unlike me. She kept me connected with the world beyond the confines of our daily routine.

"Okay," I said lowly because my throat was too tight.

"Things changed career-wise for us, Kit Kat. But we're always going to be in each other's lives."

I grimaced. "I hope so."

She put an arm around me, then we leaned our heads against each other.

"I know so," she said.

Right on cue, Kirk stopped the car along the curb of a large house not far away from the mansion where the masquerade party had taken place.

"How in the world can she afford this house?" I asked, marveling at the sheer size and scope of it. It was a white stone mansion with large trimmed trees. The landscaping alone had to cost an arm and leg.

"Oh, you didn't know," Zara said.

She had my complete attention, and I was pretty sure it showed in my expression. "Courtney's been married twice to two very rich guys. I don't know what they did for a living, but the first husband bought her the house. And when she married the second husband, the alimony stopped from the first husband, but the second was richer than the first. The second guy supposedly cheated on her with another guy, but he gave her whatever she asked for so that she wouldn't out him. But the fact that I'm telling you this story means that at some point, Courtney wagged her tongue. Because no one would ever have known the guy was gay unless Courtney told."

I belly laughed so hard that my cheeks ached. Even Kirk chuckled.

"Are you beautiful ladies ready to exit?" Kirk asked.

"Yes, but we can …"

Before I could finish, he was out and opening the door for us. I was about to tell him we could've done it ourselves.

For a moment, I caught the steady eye contact

between Zara and Kirk before she looked off bash-fully. Regardless, I asked him if he would be picking up Jake later, and he said he would be.

Before Zara and I started up the pathway, which was lit with bulbous lanterns that were staked into the grass, she waved goodbye to him, and he waved back.

"What's going on between you and Kirk?" I asked as we walked with our arms linked.

"Nothing," she said as though she were a kid caught with her hand in the candy jar.

"I'm not blind, Zara. I can clearly see the two of you flirting. Is it the fact that he's a driver?" I asked.

"Pshaw," she said, jerking her head back. "I'm not a snob. You know that."

About six people were hanging out on the large porch, very interested in our approach.

"But is that his name? Kirk?" she asked.

I flinched. "Damn it, I didn't introduce the two of you. That was a total miss on my part."

"It's fine. No need to beat yourself up about it." She stopped walking, and I followed suit. "But now that it's just the two of us, tell me, how rich is Jake Sparrow?"

I sighed then pursed my lips, pondering whether answering would betray Jake's trust.

"I mean, if he's going to send you to a party in a limousine, one that will be attended by the nosiest people at the hospital, then apparently he's not trying to be cautious," Zara said.

I shook a finger. "True."

"Okay, so what's the answer?"

I rolled my eyes. "Are you sure you wouldn't rather be a lawyer? You're so good at making your case."

She scrunched her face playfully. "Stop stalling, Penina."

I sighed. "Jake is very rich."

"How rich is very rich?"

I shook my head as if offended. "What do you mean, 'how rich'? Do you think I'd ask him where he gets his money?"

Zara grinned goofily. "Yes." Then she studied me with one eye narrowed. "Oh, that's right. No, *you* wouldn't."

We laughed.

"He just took me by surprise," Zara said as our laughter simmered.

I frowned. "Who?"

"Kirk, the driver. He's very handsome. Kind of sexy. No, really sexy."

"Should I formally introduce the two of you?"

We both turned to look at the car, and Kirk was standing against the passenger-side door, watching us—or more like watching Zara.

Zara's eyes narrowed seductively as she continued watching him. "He's a big boy. If he wants a formal introduction with me, he should know how to make one himself."

I nodded. "True."

"Anyway, so how is he in bed?" she asked.

I knew who she was talking about. The question remained stuck in my mind as I closed my eyes and let it sit there. Then the tears rushed to my eyes.

"What is it?" She sounded sorry she'd made me sad.

"Nothing. It's just ..." I sniffed and wiped my eyes.

"Is that you, Penina?" a recognizable male voice called.

Zara and I turned to the porch. Rich was leaning on the banister, holding a beer in front of his lips.

"You chose to wear that dress?" he griped.

Zara and I widened our eyes at each other.

"What's wrong with your dress?" she muttered, trying to keep her lips from moving as much as she could.

I shook my head softly as I rolled my eyes.

"Oh boy, let the games begin," she whispered as we walked forward.

FOR THE FIRST TIME SINCE WE'D BROKEN UP, I WAS happy that Rich had made an appearance. I could say for certain that I had been on the verge of confessing to Zara that Jake and I might be related. I wasn't sure I would've gone as far as to tell her everything, but Zara was too clever, and the more I talked, the closer she came to coaxing the truth out of me.

Once we were close enough, Rich glared at my tits then my face, making me feel as if I should cross my arms over my cleavage. I wanted to explain that I was dressed classy but sexy for another man, not him. But then I thought I shouldn't feel bashful or inappropriate because he was still turned on by me. He'd ruined our relationship. He was the cheater. Then he'd started a relationship with Courtney. Screw him.

I stood tall as Zara and I walked up the steps.

"And how are you tonight, Rich?" Zara asked as we were passing him.

He snarled at her and chugged his beer.

"What a tool," she whispered in my ear.

"And not the sharpest one in the shed," I muttered.

Courtney's house smelled of potpourri mixed with incense. There were a lot of furniture pieces in every visible area. It was all tied together by the same sort of lacquered cherrywood, gold-leaf trim, and silk cushions. I was standing under one of two crystal chandeliers. Zara and I were still in the foyer. There was another enormous chandelier in the living room. And every shelf, cabinet, and table had some sort of expensive knickknack on the surface. Plus, the brocade curtains had gold tassels. *Of course, the brocade curtains have gold tassels.* Her taste was just as gaudy as I knew it would be.

"There you are," a high-pitched voice squealed from somewhere amongst all the bodies.

Zara and I looked at each other with wide eyes then grinned.

Suddenly, Courtney appeared, making a path between two groups of tall, athletic men who were ogling Zara and me as if we were buck naked.

"Oh, Zara, you're back. Glad you came," Courtney said excitedly as they hugged.

"I talked to you last night, remember? You called and asked if I was coming," Zara said.

"Oh," she said, feigning as though she'd just recalled that tidbit. "Right." She hugged me. "But, Penina, Greg's here, and he's been asking about you since he arrived."

I ruffled my eyebrows at her. Frankly, I was speechless, until I wasn't. "I told you I wasn't interested in being Greg Carroll's date."

"He's nice," she squealed. "You'll like him."

"I'm going to go mingle while Court tries to set you up with another winner," Zara whispered into my ear.

I caught myself before I rolled my eyes. Since Jake had pointed the habit out to me, I was dead set on controlling it.

"What did she say?" Court asked, grinning uncomfortably.

I was certain that she only wanted Zara around because Zara kept rejecting being close friends with her. Courtney was one of those women who hated being told no, which was why I had to get something straight with her.

I put my hand on her nimble shoulder. "Court,

I'm not in the market for a boyfriend." I made sure I got very close to articulate the second part of what I had to say, because I was sure she needed to hear it. "Nor am I interested in your boyfriend."

The back of her hand shot up so fast in front of my face that I had to lean away to keep her from hitting me. "You mean my fiancé, and I know you're not interested in Rich, and he's not interested in you either." It was amazing how she said all of that in her I'm-a-nice-Valley-girl and peppy-cheerleader tone of voice.

"Good," I said, not in the least bit insulted by her need to claim Rich as her fiancé and pretend that he wasn't still in love—perhaps it was more lust —with me. I nodded while examining the room. "You have a nice turnout, though."

There were more athletes than I could count in the large room as well as the women that sniffed their tails. When Rich and I had been together, I learned that being a groupie was a full-time job. Those girls followed players from city to city, hooking up with them behind their girlfriends' and wives' backs. I was certain Rich had screwed his share of those career-athlete chasers. He probably had a steady diet of banging two a day. I patted myself on the back for caring enough about myself to make him wear a condom every time we had sex. However, Rich was right to accuse me of being the one responsible for our sex life dwindling to nonexistence. The more he'd cheated, the less attracted to him I became.

However, athletes and groupies weren't the only guests. Of course, lots of people were from the hospital, including Angela, who waved at me wildly when I spotted her. I waved back just as enthusiastically. There were also people from other walks of life, which included the worlds of entertainment and business. I knew that because I'd seen them at other functions. They were mostly Rich's friends.

"So how are you anyway?" Court asked, forcing small talk.

I wondered why she was still beside me and not mingling with other newcomers. "I'm fine." I located the group I wanted to go chat with, my entire team of residents, who looked to be having a laughing good time discussing whatever they were talking about.

"Just come with me," Court said.

To my utter surprise, she latched on to my arm and dragged me in the opposite direction from where I wanted to go. She was strong for such a tiny person. I would've had to really get aggressive to resist her, and that would've caused a scene. Since it was her party, I decided to give in a little and went without a struggle.

I was in sort of a daze as I tried to think of how to get out of whatever Court had planned for me as we walked down a narrow hallway.

"Listen to me, Pen. I know what's best for you," she said, guiding me as we entered a den. There were more muscular men and sexily clad women there. "Greg!" Courtney waved a hand wildly.

A tall man, about six feet five and built like a gladiator, turned away from the doe-eyed girl he was standing close to. The woman was still flapping her eyelashes at him as he stared at me. I was shocked that he seemed happy to see me. It was as if the sight of me hypnotized him or something. His reaction was very strange, since I'd seen him only once, maybe twice before, while I was still with Rich.

My plan of action was set. Step one was to be cordial until Court left us alone. Step two was to let him down nicely then ease back into the living room to socialize with my friends.

"So, here is she is," Court said, opening her palms toward me as if she were presenting me as a gift.

"So she is," Greg said, leering at me.

I tried not to frown, but I was sure I failed. "So what's this about?" I snapped, failing at the being cordial part of step two.

"Just, uh …" Greg said as if he was lost for words. His gaze shifted to Courtney and back to me.

My eyes narrowed. Something was familiar about the way Greg was behaving. I'd seen it with patients who didn't want their loved ones to know the extent of their illnesses. But Greg had no reason to behave that way. I began to wonder if he was pacifying Courtney because he wanted to be in Rich's shoes.

Then Courtney squeezed his bicep in that hands-on way in which she flirted with men. I vaguely remembered her coming on to Jake in front of me.

"Gosh, Pen, be nicer to this handsome guy," she said then performed a hair toss and finger rake.

"You wanted to meet me?" I asked, making a split-second decision not to turn on the charm.

Greg glanced at Courtney then back at me. "Sure," he said. "I'm shocked because you're more beautiful than I remembered."

I was on the verge of graciously calling bullcrap

on that, suspecting that he hadn't remembered me at all, when Rich called, "Penina!" His hand came down on my shoulder. "Or is it Vagina?"

He was the only one who laughed at his silly joke.

Instantly, Courtney's fake grinning fizzled into a baffled frown as Rich wrapped his arms around her from behind.

"Where's the doctor?" Rich asked, slightly slurring. He was drunk, which made sense. He always drank too much when something vexed him.

"The hospital's full of doctors. Which one are you talking about?" I asked.

"The one you're sleeping with," he said.

Court's eyes grew wide with embarrassment. My jaw dropped, as I, too, was speechless.

"The guy who drives you around town in that limousine or whatever." He reached out and tapped Greg on the shoulder. "Dude, he gets way further than I ever did."

"Rich, shut up," Courtney scolded him. "You've had too much to drink." She shimmied out of his grasp. "Let's just have dinner so you can get some food in your system and sober up and stop acting like an ass."

Courtney stomped off, clapping her tiny hands

while calling for everyone to make their way to the tent in the backyard for dinner.

"Seating arrangements have already been set. Don't sit anywhere other than where you are assigned," she said.

Rich hadn't moved yet. He stood there glaring at me until Courtney came back, grabbed him by the arm, and dragged him as she had me earlier.

Greg Carroll put a hand on my waist as if he'd just taken ownership of me. "We'd better go," he said, smirking at me as if he had decided to make a play for me.

Jake was the last person who'd touched me that way, and for a second, I felt how heartbreaking it would be if, because we were related, he wouldn't be able to touch me that way ever again. Then I checked my watch. We hadn't seen each other in four hours, and I wondered whether he was still planning on showing up or if he had been thrown into surgery.

If he was coming, then I prayed he would hurry up and get there. Something told me I was in for a long, awkward, and perhaps embarrassing dinner.

Six

JAKE SPARROW/ASHER BLACKSTONE

THREE AND A HALF HOURS AGO

I loathed lying to Penina, especially since dishonesty had been a barrier in our relationship. The call I had received was not from Si. It was from my brother Spencer. I suspected Gina had given him my number. As usual, she would do anything to get on his good side. And as usual, Spencer had no problem using her to get what he wanted, and that was me.

He was the last person I wanted to see, but he wanted to discuss Pete Sykes purchasing the hospital. I also suspected that was his way of making his visit legit. What he really wanted to do was check on me. Plus, after my encounter with the clerk in the bookstore and having to wait longer before receiving the results that would confirm a biological link between Penina and me, it almost felt like great timing to finally come face-to-face with my brother.

I had sent my last text message to Penina when I was not too far away from Si's office. I could see the door. Spencer was already in there. He had flown in from New York for our meeting and planned on flying back shortly thereafter. The closer I got to my destination, the more uncomfortable I felt. If I saw Spencer, then it would mean my lengthy hiatus from the Blackstones was officially over. But when the rubber met the road, who the hell was I kidding? There was never going to be a permanent separation from my family. But what surprised me the most was how a sudden calm had fallen over me. The sound of my black sneakers hitting the floor was all I could hear. The door to Si's office was only a few steps away. I stopped and turned to look back up the hallway, marking the distance of how far I had come. I had the freedom to forget about meeting with Spencer. I could start all over again with a new name and new hospital, have my cash back in cryptocurrency by morning, and be across the Atlantic in another country by night. If I hadn't met Penina, that was exactly what I would've done—just for the hell of it, I guessed. Running had become habit. I faced the office again, then I squeezed the doorknob and turned it.

SPENCER, WHO WAS SITTING ON THE EDGE OF THE sofa, stood when he saw me. I couldn't move for a few beats. Seeing him had instantly transported me to another place and time. It wasn't good or bad, just different.

"Ash," he said.

I slowly closed the door behind me but didn't come closer. I had no idea why I stayed there unmoving, like a boulder. It wasn't as if Spencer was going to bite.

Nodding sharply, I said, "Spencer. What are you doing here?"

He sniffed as if his reason should've been obvious. "You bought a hospital under the name of Pete Sykes."

"Then you're here to check out my investment."

I waited for him to hurl a nice big insult. I wanted him to make it good, so hurtful and demeaning that it reminded me why I'd gone

73

running for the hills in the first place. So far, though, he watched me—more like examined me.

"You look good," he said finally.

I pressed my lips together, refusing to say it back, even though it was true. He looked different. Spencer's face used to have a gaunt hardness about it but not anymore. It was as if something evil that used to burden him had released him, setting his soul free.

"You mentioned Pete Sykes," I said, attempting to sound like less of a jerk. "Is he retired or something?"

Spencer snorted a chuckle. "No, he isn't. But with Father gone, he's not operating in the background anymore." Spencer touched himself on the chest. "My company, TFC Global, is now under the umbrella of Blackstone Family Enterprises." He grinned as if he was proud of it and wanted me to be too.

I jerked my head back. "No way?"

His grin got bigger. "Yeah, way."

Even though we maintained a safe distance, we shared chortles.

"Congratulations," I said.

"Thank you. My wife gave me a surprise party and everything," Spencer said, simpering. "It was nice."

I could feel my eyes constrict as I tried to figure out if that was really my obnoxious brother standing in front of me.

"I'm glad you're doing well, though, Ash. Let's sit and talk about some things."

Spencer had always been big on power games. One of them was never to sit before the person he was in a meeting with had. In his mind, the first person to take a seat relinquished the power. So I waited for him to pause, but he didn't. He sat first, and I was shocked as hell.

"Your wife, huh?" I asked as I took the seat in the armchair across from him.

Spence was still smiling. "Yeah. She's too good for me, but I do my best."

I was confused about what sort of woman would marry Spencer, especially given the relationship he had with Gina.

"I can tell by that look on your face that you have doubts about that," he said.

I grunted. Since he'd mentioned it, I figured I had a license to be honest. "I recall you liked to hit, draw blood, and bruises…"

Spence nodded thoughtfully then took a deep

breath as he sat up straight. "Remember that thera-pist I referred to you?"

"Karma or something like that," I said.

"Dr. Mita Sharma. She's excellent. She gave me what I needed to change my life," he said with the same peaceful grin.

I studied how relaxed and in control of his being Spencer was, then stroked my chin. "Indeed, she is excellent," I said thoughtfully.

My brother and I observed each other for a moment longer until he shifted abruptly.

"And you're a surgeon, huh?" he asked, grin-ning again.

I tilted my head curiously. "You really didn't know?"

Spencer threw his hands up as she shook his head. "You wanted your space, so Jasper, Bryn, and I gave it to you."

I didn't know what to think of that. For the longest time, I'd thought they expended a lot of energy trying to find me. That was why I'd gone to Australia. I'd always been careful about keeping my false identity secure. Lately, I'd been sloppy, though, and I suspected subconsciously that had been on purpose.

"But listen, I want to talk about what you

bought here," Spencer said.

I pressed my lips together as I bounced my knee. I wasn't sure if I was ready to discuss business. I needed a moment. Something about the way he sat there, pulled together, healthy, happy, and living life as if we hadn't come from the same place, annoyed me. The fact that he could get to that point without hitting the road made no sense at all.

"All this time, you stuck around the family and the business and—"

"No, I didn't. I got the hell away from there too. I didn't go as far as you did, but I went away for a while. Bought the ranch in Wyoming, and the rest is history." He was grinning again as he relaxed against the sofa and folded his fingers behind his head. It was as though he'd forgotten that he'd tried to usher me into a conversation that focused solely on business.

I figured that while he made himself comfortable, I might as well get to my biggest request before we started in on discussing the hospital. I abruptly crossed and uncrossed my legs, still unable to make myself as relaxed as he had. "Listen, Spence, I have a friend. She took a DNA test and was flagged by your foundation."

He sat up straight again. "Is that so?" He

sounded genuinely interested in what I was saying. *Who the hell is this guy?*

"Yes," I said.

"What's her name?"

I hesitated.

Spencer stretched his neck from side to side. For the first time, I saw that he was just as uncomfortable about the meeting as I was.

"Ash, you can trust me. I'm giving you my best here. I know we haven't been the friendliest of brothers. But I love you and always have, and always will," he said.

I nodded continuously. I loved him, too, and always had and always would. "Her name is Penina Ross," I said finally.

Spencer raised a finger as he took his cell phone out of his pocket. "Give me a second." He placed a call and looked off as he waited for someone to answer. "Babe, it's me." His grin formed slowly. "Yeah, I'm here." He glanced at me. "He's here too. Listen, can you look up Penina Ross in the indemnity fund database?" He paused. "Yes, for payouts."

Spencer winked at me, which clued me in to how intensely I was studying him. I'd always loved him, but for the first time in our lives, I liked this new brother of mine. His presence also showed me how different I was too. On the day my father died, my siblings and I hadn't sat around grieving. We all got the hell away from each other as fast as we could. It suddenly dawned on me that we couldn't have remained around each other and matured. There was no faster way to clear a room than putting Bryn, Spencer, Jasper, and me around a dinner table. We behaved like toddlers. Even though our father was dead, we still had to run away from the expectations Randolph had for us. The man had been absent most of our lives, yet his demands were like constant nooses around all of our necks.

"Thanks, babe," Spencer said finally. "See you soon."

Then he told the other person he loved her, and it sank in that he worked with his wife.

"Penina Ross is the daughter of Arthur Valentine. Does she work here at the hospital?" Spencer asked.

"Yes," I said before I realized it. Then I balled up my fist and pressed my knuckles to my teeth. It took every bit of willpower not to reschedule our meeting, get the hell to that party as fast as I could, break the news to Penina, then take her back to the penthouse and make to her in every which way I knew how.

"Good news, huh?" Spencer said, smirking.

Damn, I was still grinning from ear to ear as I looked my brother in the eye. He'd said I could trust him. He could probably see from the stupid look on my face that I was in love. It felt natural to keep Penina to myself or else risk her being stolen by Spencer or Jasper. But if I wanted my world to be different with my family in it, then I had to operate differently.

"Penina is a surgeon in the hospital. She's beautiful woman on the inside and out. I'm crazy about," I admitted.

Spence tossed his head back. "Ah, I see. No wonder you asked me right up front. Is that why you showed up?"

"Sort of. I also wanted to see you," I was happy to admit.

Spence stood and held his arms out. "Then can I finally get a hug?"

I grunted as I leapt to my feet. Then we bear-hugged each other. It felt good to be in my brother's life again.

"I need to talk to you about one more thing," he said.

I was still at ease with him, but I could tell that the other shoe was about to drop.

"What is it?" I asked.

"Did you and Bryn put Father out of his misery?"

We sat down again.

I rubbed the tension out of the back of my neck. Frankly, the business of Bryn and I snuffing our father out was coming up way too much for my comfort. "Have you spoken to Bryn?"

"Yes," he said, nodding firmly.

I scratched my forehead. "And what did she say?"

"Bryn said she can't talk about it without you."

I pushed my shoulders back. "And I can't say anything without her." Our pact was childish, that was for sure, but my sister and I had made a deal never to talk about what happened before our father took his last breath without the other's permission.

Spencer grunted. He was used to Bryn and me sticking together. "I guess we have to get you both in the same room. But you really haven't heard what they're accusing you of?"

I was still frowning about his suggesting that he, Bryn, and I—and I was sure Jasper too—would be in the same room again. Those sorts of gatherings never went well for us.

He was still waiting for me to answer his question.

"Spence, I'm a surgeon. I spend three-quarters of my life in the OR. And the people who work in the hospital don't give care about the Blackstones."

Spencer grinned again. He looked proud. "Ash, I couldn't believe it when Si told me you were a neurosurgeon." He said "neurosurgeon" in the same tone in which he'd say I was the president of the United States or something. "You cut people's heads open and work on their brains."

I leaned away from him. "Si?"

"Yeah, I put two and two together when Pete Sykes bought the medical center where Simon Brown was chief of surgery."

I nodded. "I was sloppy then."

"Pretty much."

I shrugged, knowing I definitely could've tried harder to be cleaner. "But I thought Gina might have mentioned where I was to you." I then communicated how one of her friends had made me at Bartleby Leonard's annual masquerade party the other night—he was an associate of our family's. I relayed how I had taken the risk of going because Penina had said she hadn't had a real night on the town in a long time, and I wanted to be the one to show her some fun.

"I can understand that," Spencer said. "I spoke to Gina a few weeks ago, before I dropped out of the Senate race."

I pointed my index finger at him. "I heard you were running for the Senate. I never knew you were interested in politics."

A smirk passed across Spence's mouth, evaporating just as fast as it showed up. "I wasn't. The things we'd do for the women we love."

"Ha," I scoffed. "I can understand that."

The glint in his eyes meant he'd caught my joke. That sort of light back-and-forth banter wasn't normal for us. He would usually scowl about what I had just said, and I would give him something to really be offended about. There was never any peace in our relationship. And his negativity, and mine as well, could overpower a room and suck the oxygen and joy right out of it. So far, we were swimming in oxygen and, surprisingly, a whole lot of joy too.

Spencer stretched his arm across the top of the sofa, making himself more comfortable. "As I said before, Gina showed up at my office in New York. I hadn't seen her in years. She looked good, though. Teaching young girls how to be Olympic champions seems to be agreeing with her."

He spoke of Gina as if they were old friends. I remembered them as two people who used to beat the crap out of each other and get off on it. I'd peeked in on them once. Gina egged Spencer on to hit her. At first, he shrank away from her, but she insulted him, calling him no good, trash, using words that would make Spencer angry enough to haul off and hit her. Their relationship was built on sickness, but he spoke as if they were neighbors on Mr. Rogers's block.

"So how did it go between the two of you?" I asked to get at the truth.

Spencer shifted out of his comfortable position and fidgeted until he rounded his shoulders and sank deeper into the cushion. "One of my political opponents was attempting to blackmail her. I handled it. Sure, she said she loved me. But I'm in love with my wife and faithful to her."

It was still difficult to picture Spencer having a typical relationship with anyone.

"How's your relationship with your wife?" I asked, and I instantly wished I hadn't. A man's wife was his refuge. I was being critical of him, and Spencer knew me well enough to understand it.

He sniffed. "My relationship with my wife is good," he said, nodding. "Healthy." He tilted his head as he paused. "I would like for you to meet her —soon."

I nodded, watching him study my reaction. Spencer was testing me to see if I was ready to return to the fold.

I rubbed the wrinkles out of my forehead. "Sure, one day, yeah."

"How's your relationship with Penina Ross?" he asked.

I smiled because the mention of her name made me feel good from the inside out. "It's healthy, too, and fun."

"Fun?" Spencer asked, nodding as if he liked the sound of that. "You're too serious to have fun."

I snorted a chuckle. "The scalpel changed me. Once I was able to transfer my need to control everything that could go awry into operating on my patients and saving their lives, I could be looser about everything else."

Spencer stretched the sides of his mouth downward, continuing to nod thoughtfully. "I get it."

I narrowed my eyes doubtfully. "Do you?" The

brother I'd once known had no time or patience for complex principles of life.

"Yeah," he said as if it was obvious that he had understood what I meant. "I had to transfer my anger into retribution for what Father and Valentine did to those girls, and even what Father did to us. If it weren't for Jasper taking the lead, you, Bryn, and I would no doubt be messed up beyond repair."

I glared at the floor as Spencer scowled at the wall. We let silence sit for a moment. Captured in the space of time was true appreciation for our older brother constantly protecting us, watching out for us like a hawk.

Finally, Spencer smiled faintly. "But listen, Ash." His tone indicated a change in subject. Then his smile grew as he reached out to take me by the shoulder nearest him and shook me as if we were celebrating a winning touchdown or something. "How the hell were you able to acquire this hospital? We didn't know it was for sale. No one did. And we've been trying to purchase a medical facility just like this one for our portfolio."

I put my hands up, palms facing him. "Wait a minute. This is my operation. It's not going to be a cash cow for BFE."

Spencer shook his head. "It'll make money, but

that won't be its only purpose. We do it differently now that Father's gone and all his cronies aren't affiliated with our business anymore. Jasper cleaned house real good."

Then he explained how he and his wife were about to go on a world tour, finding partners to expand their foundation. They wanted to build a wing onto the hospital to provide free top-notch medical services for people who had been victims of sex trafficking.

I was blown away by everything he told me. Not in a million years would I have thought Spencer would care about anyone more than he did himself.

Then he asked me to explain to "us" how I had come across the purchase.

"Us?" I asked.

He picked up his cell phone and shook it.

I grimaced at his device while saying, "Si's on the board. They wanted to keep their money problems quiet. Si said he could probably bring them a discreet buyer. A few days later, he pitched their proposal to me." I smirked, remembering the next part. "I asked myself, 'What would Jasper do in this scenario?' That was when I used the Pete Sykes credentials to make all inquiries about the purchase. I was shocked it was still active, and Jasper hadn't been alerted. I had the cash. I offered them a price, and we negotiated a few numbers before they accepted my best and final one."

"Did you hear that, Jasper?" Spencer asked.

"Every word," Jasper said, his voice projecting through Spencer's cell phone.

Hearing him made my throat tighten. I never realized how much I missed my brothers. In one sense, it was as if we hadn't gone a day without speaking to or seeing each other. But on the other hand, it was clear time spent apart was the reason I felt that way.

I could feel how widely I was smiling, though. "Jasper, how are you?" I asked past my thick throat.

Jasper coughed. "I'm well, Ash. I'm happy as hell to be talking to you too. It's been too long. Let me ask you something, though."

I sat up straight. "Shoot."

"Are you ready to join us again? If not, it's fine. But if you are, then we should get right down to business."

I rubbed my jaw, then the back of my neck, until I realized why I was stalling—then I stopped.

I knew what getting down to business entailed. I would have to put Jake Sparrow to rest and become Asher Nathaniel Blackstone again. Spencer was watching me closely, and Jasper's curiosity hung in the air. I shifted uncomfortably in my seat and did more on-the-spot soul-searching. Then, suddenly, I was struck by illumination.

Our father was dead. I recalled the last time my siblings and I were together. The bickering and lack of respect was excessive. I was part of it, and I'd hated my participation in it then, and I hated it now. The interesting part was that all of us, excluding Jasper, had to go off on our own and grow up. As usual, our older brother held down the fort. Now that I had some tools to withstand the hard parts as well the easier parts of being a Blackstone, it was time I pulled my weight.

So I took a deep breath, braced myself for all of what was to come next, and spoke my answer.

Seven

⚬⚬⚬

PENINA ROSS

On the way to the backyard, Greg Carroll softly took me by the arm and whispered, "Actually, I do want to talk to you about something."

I assessed his expression. His gaze flitted around the space, checking out nearby faces.

"About what?" I asked, sensing I was supposed to keep my voice down.

"You're a neurosurgeon." He wasn't asking. He already knew.

I nodded.

"I have a problem that I need to talk to a neurologist about—one not associated with my team or that is within my organization's reach. Is that you, Dr. Penina Ross?"

Then my gaze flitted around Court's overly designed room. "You want to talk privately?" I asked after my eyes landed back on him.

He nodded and led me in the opposite direction of where everyone else was going. Greg held the front door open for me to walk out onto the patio first. Then he checked behind him and stepped outside too. I folded my arms, feeling uneasy about all the secrecy. It was weird. But Greg wasn't done being paranoid as he searched to the right of the house then the left of it.

"This way," he said and started down the stairs, searching every dark space as he went.

I wondered what made him so distrustful. He was beginning to worry me, but I followed him until we stopped under a healthy tree with wiry branches that draped over the lawn enough to provide us some cover.

"Are you going to tell me what's going on now?" I asked, frowning curiously and making sure to put enough distance between us that I could slip away from him if he tried to grab me. He hadn't earned my full trust yet. As long as he was behaving as if we were in the middle of a drug deal, I had to be cautious.

"I was hit last year, hard," he whispered. "When

I slammed into the ground, I passed out, but nobody saw what happened. The cameras didn't even capture the aftermath, and I was told not to mention it."

I slapped at an insect that landed on my shoulder. "Okaaay …"

"I saw our doctor. They told me everything looked fine, but I don't think it's true." He shook his head.

"Why not?" I asked, rubbing my arms, trying to keep another bug from landing on me.

"I've been forgetting big things, small things, everything and getting massive headaches."

"Since last year?"

He frowned thoughtfully. "I don't know. I've had headaches ever since I started playing this game. But for the past few weeks, I've been having bouts of memory lapse that I've never had before."

"Well, if the impact was a year ago—"

"I don't trust them. I know they're not telling me the truth."

I searched his eyes. He looked desperate for answers. If he was reporting symptoms now, it didn't necessarily mean they weren't related to what happened to him back then. Something buzzed past my ear, and I twisted a finger inside it. I really wanted to go back inside and cool off, but I had to put my doctor's hat on, which meant listening to him intently. "Can you give me an example of what you have been forgetting?"

His Adam's apple bobbed as he gulped. "Sometimes my name."

"Oh." I hadn't expected him to say that.

His eyes expanded so wide that I could see the white around the iris. "Like for real. I can forget my name. My address too." He scratched his temple. "Sometimes I even forget where I am."

I touched him gently on the shoulder. "Can you come to the hospital tomorrow for tests?"

"No," he whispered curtly. Greg checked over both shoulders. "They're watching me."

"Who's watching you?"

"I'm guaranteed thirty-five million dollars on a three-year contract, as long as I'm stopping a quarterback from scoring touchdowns. They want me to play until I die, and that's no joke."

"I see," I said. "Well, if I don't run scans, then I can't learn what's wrong with you."

He scratched his head as his frown intensified. "Listen, let me figure it out and get back to you."

I nodded, thankful that we were coming to the end of my spur-of-the-moment consultation for

Greg Carrol while getting eaten alive by mosquitoes. "I'm at the hospital in the morning. I'll also speak to a colleague of mine, and we'll figure something out."

He nodded. "Thank you."

We swapped numbers and headed inside. Greg waited for me in the hallway while I went into the guest bathroom to wash my hands. He asked me where I was from and how long I'd been in New Orleans as we walked to the backyard, where Courtney had a monstrous tent set up on the lawn. The inquiries into my personal life stopped once we stepped inside the tarp. Thank goodness she had the sense to make it air-conditioned. *Yay, Court!*

Greg and I stopped and searched from one corner to the other. Tables were along the canvas walls, which held strings of twinkling lights above the diners' heads. There had to be over a hundred people in that massive tent. Also, bulbous paper pendant lights looked as if they floated in thin air throughout. I had to get a closer look to see the translucent string holding them in place. There was also a dance floor in the middle and a platform for a band on one side of the space.

"There they are," Courtney called. She was

sitting next to Rich, who was looking at us as if he wanted to take our heads off.

I was very aware that she was hyperfocused on me, and it made me uneasy. Suddenly, it felt wrong to be a guest at the party of my ex-boyfriend, who I was not on good terms with, and his mousy new girlfriend. If I weren't waiting for Jake to show up, I would've feigned not feeling well and had Kirk take me home.

"Over there," Courtney said, pointing as far away from her and Rich as she could and certainly out of her boyfriend's line of sight.

I performed a quick search for Zara as I walked to where Courtney was directing us. Not only was she nowhere to be found, but I also remembered that Courtney had made her own seating arrangement, and I didn't have to be a brain surgeon to guess who I was seated beside.

I so very badly wanted to take Courtney by the shoulders, shake her, and tell her that if she was that insecure about her relationship with Rich, then she should probably do what I had done and dump him. However, Courtney's love life wasn't any of my concern. Greg and I smiled faintly at each other and sat down. But then I remembered I was supposed to save Jake a seat next to me. I searched up and down my side of the table—there were no empty chairs. However, when I zeroed in on Court, there were two empty chairs to her left. One of those seats must've belonged to Jake and the other to Zara.

I heaved a sigh, considering shifting Courtney's seating chart. But I couldn't. That sort of rudeness wasn't my style. So I decided to make the best out of an infuriating situation.

First, everyone was served drinks and crawfish-and-crab-cake appetizers. They tasted horrible—too fishy and salty. I took one bite and no more. I was pretty sure Greg was happy that we were sandwiched between people who worked at the hospital because he asked me to tell him everything I knew about CTE. I took care to keep my voice low as I explained. And we probably appeared intimate to those who watched us with curious gazes. That was probably why I felt Jake's presence before I saw him or heard Crystal Collins from obstetrics and gynecology whisper his name to Dorothy, one of her colleagues.

Jake was standing at the entrance of the tent when our eyes connected. I felt my smile steadily grow, a natural reaction roused from within me on seeing his gorgeous face. But I was the only one beaming. Jake did not look happy as his frown shifted between Greg and me.

"Dr. Sparrow. You made it," Courtney sang. "You're sitting over here by me."

I wanted to strangle her.

"So do you think I have it?" Greg asked, not noticing me staring at Jake.

I knew I was looking longingly after him because I felt it on my face. "I don't know. We'll have to test for it," I said, watching Jake sit down.

He wasn't looking at me anymore, and I wondered if it was because he thought I had transferred my affections to Greg Carroll.

I turned back to Greg. "Actually, the doctor who just walked in is one of the best neurosurgeons in the world."

Funny, but he looked right at Jake. I hadn't thought Greg noticed him.

Greg grunted. "I heard you were pretty good."

I nodded. "I am."

"But you're the only one I can trust."

"You can trust any doctor to keep your care confidential."

"And I'm trusting you to keep my care confidential."

I studied his grin with narrowed eyes then

leaned back once I realized we were again appearing too intimate.

"He's your boyfriend or your colleague?" Greg asked, eyeing Jake.

I whipped my face around to see Jake practically snarling at us. "Either that or my brother."

Greg chuckled at my delivery. He had to know the context to get my joke, and there was no way I was explaining it to him.

Suddenly, Courtney sprang to her feet. "Thank you all for coming to our Midsummer's Eve party. We're going to have a lot of fun. By the way, Rich and I are getting married."

That time, she stretched her arm out, flashing her ring to everyone in the tent, and applause erupted all around us. Heck, I clapped too. The two of them more than likely deserved each other. Jake didn't clap. He looked miserable sitting beside her, staring. He was probably upset that he'd asked me to save him a seat beside me and I hadn't. I wanted to, though.

Finally, it quieted down.

"For dinner, we're going to have some good old-fashioned gumbo and jambalaya," she announced, sounding more like a Valley girl than ever.

I tried to avoid Jake's cold stare.

"JJ Good is in the house."

She clapped, and applause erupted again as a guy with curly hair and a pointy goatee stood up and took a bow. He was wearing tight pants that were rolled up above his ankles and a red velvet vest that showed off his hilly chest and biceps.

Courtney then pushed out her hip, posing. "So, all y'all are going to get to see my lady parts tonight. JJ's going to paint me nude, live! But don't worry, I'm not going to show anything you all haven't seen before."

"Girl, I didn't come here to see your twiggy little ass," a guy who looked like a football player said.

"Screw you, Damon," Courtney retorted.

Damon clapped and laughed. She rolled her eyes. That was one thing I liked about Court—she knew how to react to a joke when she heard one.

"But first," she announced like a whiny little ringmaster. "It's time for midsummer-night fairies!" She clapped excitedly, and everyone couldn't help but join her.

Music started outside the tent, then in danced six nearly naked girls with flowing scarves tied around their heads, their breasts fully exposed, bushy pussies fully out too.

A laugh escaped me as a band of flute players

comprising shirtless guys with long wigs and pieces of cloth over their loins followed the girls. I bit down on my bottom lip to keep myself from cracking up. I couldn't decide whether the performance was tasteless or just plain old foolish. Thank goodness Zara wasn't around, or we would've inappropriately broken out in laughter together. When my amused eyes found Jake's, he pointed his head toward the exit and lifted an eyebrow.

I nodded eagerly, and after he stood, I turned to say goodnight to Greg. I knew I wouldn't be back, but he was enthralled by the dancing titties. So I got up, and keeping eye contact with Jake, I walked with him toward the exit.

My attention was diverted when Rich shot to his feet as well. I couldn't believe he was following Jake around the table. He would've made it all the way if Courtney hadn't run after him. When Jake and I made it out of the tent, he took my hand and guided me as far away from the noise as he could.

We stopped next to a lit swimming pool that had candles floating on top of the water. Courtney had thought of everything in her effort to impress her guests.

Jake and I beamed at each other. I couldn't help myself as I cradled one side of his face in the palm of my hand. But instead of kissing him, I cleared my throat and dropped my arm to my side.

"Courtney had assigned seating, and she wanted you all to herself."

Jake pointed his head toward the tent. "What's up with that guy, anyway? I'm starting believe you're not safe around him."

"Don't worry about Rich. He's a harmless meathead who doesn't like to lose."

He shrugged. "I'm not faulting the guy for being sour. If I had you and lost you, I'd be angry too."

I sniffed, looking down bashfully. When I looked up again, we stared into each other's eyes for a prolonged period of time. I felt as if my heart would explode. He'd been out of my presence for nearly six hours, and it felt more like six months.

Suddenly, his lips moved toward mine, and I placed my fingers in front of my mouth.

"Jake," I said, warning him.

"Penina."

My eyes fluttered closed to allow that dizzy feeling that occurred whenever he said my name that way to pass. "We can't," I said, allowing my eyes to softly open again.

My mouth was caught open as his finger trailed

down my cleavage, sliding over my erect nipple so that his hand could grip my waist and draw me against him. "I'm not your brother."

Breathe, Penina. "Then you've gotten the results?" I sounded winded.

"Yes, I have. We're not related."

I gasped. "No?"

He shook his head. "No."

"You sure?"

"I'm positive."

Then our lips melted into each other. The delicious taste of his mouth, his strong and eager tongue, were driving me wild with lust. I grabbed Jake—or Asher—by the lapel of his crisp white shirt and jammed my mouth harder against his. The sexy sensation of his tongue hungrily circling mine made my head spin.

"Let's get out of here," he said breathlessly.

"Dr. Sparrow, Penina?"

I recognized the voice. We turned to see Deb watching us from a distance. She seemed out of place standing where she was. I guessed she had inched her way over to where we were to identify the impassioned kissers.

"Deb?" I asked, catching my breath.

"Good night, Dr. Glasgow," Jake said, tugging me along.

I felt as if I needed to explain what she'd seen. However, my feet were determined to keep pace with Jake, and soon I chose to forget all about being in trouble with Deb for the night. I would deal with her in the morning.

We trotted across the lawn. I felt as if I were running on air. Every now and then, we stopped at a tree and made out profusely. We moved a little farther toward the front of the house, and he pulled the fabric of my dress from over my right breast and sank my nipple and as much of my flesh as he could into the warm, wet concaves of his mouth.

"Mm." He grasped my waist and sucked on my tits more fervently. "Do you know how sexy you look in this dress?" he asked.

He put his mouth back on mine as the warm air of night cooled my wet nipples. Jake bent me backward, kissing me deeply. Finally, almost abruptly, he forced himself to gain control of his lust. I had done the same, only my head felt as if it were floating away from my shoulders as we made it to the front of the house and back to the limo.

. . .

THE WINDOW'S UP, THE ONE SEPARATING THE FRONT from the back. Positioning himself between my thighs, Jake lowers me. We stare deep into each other's eyes as my back presses against the spacious, soft leather seat.

His eyes narrow just a pinch. Our heavy breaths clash.

"How dare you make me wait to do this?" he says, then his tongue invades my mouth again. I whimper as his full-grown erection digs against my soaked panties.

He touches me down there, and I stiffen. In and out, he's fingering me. My senses are on overload. I'm about to blow a gasket.

"You're so wet. I want to … damn!" he shouts, lifting my dress, letting the hem bunch on my sternum.

He's fast, snatching my panties off. Possessed by lust, he presses his shoulders under my thighs, lowering his face to my sex. Then …

"Ahh!" I cry.

His tongue stimulates my pleasure spot, instantly sending orgasmic streaks through me.

When he plunges his tongue in and out of my wetness, the erotic sensation makes me shudder.

"Oh, Jake," I sigh.

His tongue is an expert, diving in and out of me, around my clit, bringing me close then pulling back by sinking inside me again, then back on the clit, building sensations, making me ready.

I squeeze my eyes tighter and clench my teeth harder.

It's …

"J …"

Stronger.

"Oh G …"

I slap my hands against the top and edge of the seat.

"Ah!" I cry for dear life as the most pleasurable feeling known to woman spreads through me.

I'm on sensory overload when Jake loosens his belt, unzips, and frees his bountiful cock.

Through my hooded eyes, I admire how engorged it is. Before I can reach out and feel it, he puts himself between my thighs.

He shudders as his cock surges through me.

He pumps, making me feel so damn good. Then he halts abruptly.

I stop sucking air and open my eyes. He's looking at me.

"WHAT?" I WHISPERED. I WAS EAGER FOR HIM TO get going again. I was close to feeling the intravaginal orgasm that I found addictingly pleasurable.

"I wasn't in surgery earlier," he said as if he was straining to talk.

My eyebrows pulled together. "Okay."

"I was in a meeting with my brothers."

"Okay."

I cracked a smile while rubbing the layer of glistening sweat off his forehead. "It's just that I'm about to come already …"

We both were careful not to move so much while we chuckled.

"Your brothers, huh?" I asked, trying to stave off our need for each other long enough for him to gain control of his desire.

He closed his eyes, nodding. "Mm-hm."

But our lips, having other plans, sensually stroked each other, then our tongues.

"Damn, you taste so sweet." He sighed then said, "Hear me out."

"I'm listening." I grunted then bit down on my lower lip as Jake's cock stroked me.

His breaths trembled as they slid out of his nose. "I bought the hospital." He winced.

My eyes opened wide. *Did I hear him right?*

His shifted me faster. "On Monday, I'll make the announcement."

"What announcement?" I strained to ask.

"That Blackstone Family Enterprise owns the hospital, and my real name is Asher Nathaniel Blackstone."

It wasn't fair that he wanted to have that

conversation while we were doing that. To keep him quiet, I thrust my tongue deep into his mouth and kissed him intensely.

Even though I had tons of questions to ask him about buying the hospital, I was feeling him again, and he felt so damn good.

I gasped. He gasped.

Each thrust stimulated a new orgasm.

One.

Two.

Three.

Four.

"Oh, baby!" Jake's body quaked as he erupted.

HE HAD FLIPPED ME OVER TO LIE ON TOP OF HIM AS we both cooled down. I kissed him tenderly on the lips then the tip of his nose.

"Mmm ..." he moaned.

We smiled at each other.

"Sorry I couldn't hold on for you, babe. I'll make it up to you later."

I smiled with bliss. "We have all night, don't we?"

He trailed a finger across my lower lip. "Yes, we do."

There was no time better than the present to address his confessions. "So you met with your brothers today. You own the hospital, and you're letting everyone who works there—"

Suddenly, his cell phone dinged. It was on the floor. Instinctively, we both turned to look and see who it was. A text message was pasted on the screen.

It's Julia. Miss me? I miss you, sexy.

My mouth fell open. Then came the question I never wanted to ask about another woman when a man was still inside me.

"Who's Julia?"

Eight

PENINA ROSS

We were still in the back of the limousine, being chauffeured through the steamy New Orleans night. I was no longer on top of Jake, straddling his hips while he was inside me. My lust was cooling, but his was not as he continued rubbing my inner thigh. I didn't mind his hand on me, even though I was slightly pissed that he admitted that the flirty text came from my sister by blood, Julia Valentine.

"I still don't understand why you didn't say something about her being your ex-girlfriend beforehand," I had said.

He sighed. "I apologize. I should've said something."

"Yes, you should've."

"I know but—" He massaged his temples with his thumbs.

"Do you still love her?" I had asked, frowning. I sensed his inner turmoil had something to do with the way he felt about her.

He shook his head adamantly. "No way."

"Then why is she getting to you this way?"

He had told me their relationship was toxic. They would hurt each other for sport. He didn't love her. He couldn't love her. They were together just to make each other miserable.

We stared into each other's eyes, letting his confession sink in. Jake refused to reply to Julia's first and very long text message. In an act of absolute transparency, he read it aloud. Julia mentioned how much she missed him and hoped he missed her too. I closed my eyes and let my negative reactions flow out of my body.

"Are you okay?" he asked.

Barely, but I nodded anyway.

He rubbed my thigh and squeezed it before reading on. She said his brothers had not treated her kindly in his absence, but she had forgiven them. She also said they needed to have a conversation as soon as possible. They had very important matters to discuss and pleasure to catch up on.

I couldn't stop shaking my head. How dare she be so bold with my lover? Had she believed he would sit around and wait for her forever?

Jake deleted the message, set his phone face-down on a console next to a bucket of chilled bottles of water, then wrapped his large hand around my wrist and tugged me to him.

I chose not to resist when our mouths melted. His tongue seized mine, and he lowered me down onto the long seat. I tried to focus on how delicious he tasted and his strong hands groping my breast, exposing my nipple, and then his hot mouth sucking it against his tongue. As I sizzled with erotic sensations, I tried not to focus on his cell phone beeping and vibrating. But then it rang.

All of a sudden, Jake's stimulation abandoned my body. "Damn it!" he roared as he collapsed back against the seat, rubbing his palms over his face.

The volume of his voice made me jump. "Jake," I groused.

"Sorry, babe," he muttered and then snatched his phone out of the cargo holder.

I watched in awe as he did what hospital surgeons rarely did and silenced all calls. But it had to be done. The woman had been relentless in her efforts.

My intense frown was giving me a headache. "Well, what do you think she wants?"

"Don't know. Don't care," he said as he took hold of me and guided me over to sit on his lap.

He went back to work, chomping on the tit closest to his mouth. It felt good, but I couldn't focus on the way his tongue circled my nipple before he sucked my perky breast into his mouth. Then he bit the tip.

"Ouch!" I yelped, recoiling.

"Sorry," he winced and then scrubbed his face again.

Jake looked paler and wearier than usual. It bothered me that one woman could so intensely disturb his peace of mind. He could be obsessive about his object of desire. I knew that for certain because he was that way with me. Regardless of how much it seemed he wanted to keep having sex, I couldn't help but wonder if the reappearance of Julia was making him lose interest in me.

"I just don't get it," I said, pulling my dress back over my breasts.

"You don't get what?"

"It seems as though she means a lot to you."

He blew another hard sigh as he scratched his eyebrow. "She doesn't, Penina."

"I don't believe you." I tried to slide off his lap, but he maintained a vise grip on my hips.

"Babe, come on. Don't let Julia ruin our night."

"She's not ruining our night. You are." My voice echoed through the back of the limo.

We stared at each other for several moments.

"I want to know why she still gets to you this way, that's all." I set my jaw, refusing to budge until he answered honestly.

"It's not just Julia. It's everything that happened today. Julia's just the tip of the iceberg."

My eyebrows pulled into an intense frown. "What do you mean?"

"Everything. My brothers, being Asher Blackstone again." He scoffed. "I didn't think I'd ever encounter Julia again, yet here she is, making herself front and center. That's what bothers me, Penina. That's all."

I waited for him to look at me. When he did, I nodded softly, letting him know I understood.

"Then you plan to come clean about your identity?" I asked.

His gaze ventured down to my cleavage and back to my face. "This is not supposed to be happening right now."

I knew what he meant.

"But it is happening."

He sighed. "I know. And yes, I am coming clean to all hospital personnel."

Finally, he didn't try to stop me when I scooted off his lap. I was disappointed by that. The distance between us felt like an impending threat.

Once he was free of me, he massaged his temples. Jake rarely slept, and it showed, but I'd never seen him look so ghoulish.

"And Julia Valentine doesn't inspire warm memories, you know," he added.

I nodded understandingly, trying very hard to put myself in his shoes. I had been just as angry when Rich trapped me in Dr. Best's office and tried to bang me, which was an activity he wasn't that great at, especially compared to Jake. I had felt violated and insulted because I had gotten over him, and he had the nerve to treat me as if I hadn't.

But I had to say something to convince Jake that I wasn't jealous or afraid of losing him, even though I was. "Well, then maybe you should answer her call and find out what she wants." I could hardly believe that was what I'd come up with, and I immediately wanted to take it back while at the same time allowing my words to stand.

I could see the wheels turning in Jake's mind as

he watched me with narrowed eyes. My chest was tight and my body completely still. Jake had been something very good that happened in my life, which was something that hadn't occurred in a long time.

I had sort of sworn off men after Rich. My ex-boyfriend had certainly left me bitter about finding true love, Prince Charming, and crap like that. Maybe Jake's brothers and his ex-girlfriend, who I couldn't forget was my long-lost sister, had busted our bubble at the right time. After all, our relation-ship was entering a new phase. To me, he had always been Jake Sparrow, but I had to be honest with myself. The sky-blue eyes I was looking into, the ones that had always been so intense and care-ful, belonged to a man named Asher Blackstone.

"I need to get some work done tonight," he said in a low voice. "How about I take a rain check?"

My mouth fell open. We had chosen that night to make up for being so afraid we would never be able to make love again. He was supposed to make me climax so many times that by the morning, I would feel as loose as a rag doll. Between sessions of us banging each other's brains out, I would catnap while he squeezed my tits until he turned me over so he could put them in his mouth while groping my ass and rubbing my clit. Jake loved rousing me, making it hard for me to ignore his handiwork.

So I allowed Julia Valentine that victory and quickly replaced my astonishment with a gracious smile. "Okay," I said, overly chipper.

Jake nodded as he stared into my eyes. "Thanks, Penina. And um, it's time to refer to me as Asher." He sighed. "Asher Blackstone."

I CLOSED MY EYES AS ASHER AND I KISSED. Heartbroken, I had already turned away from him when he said, "See you in the morning."

The car waited in front of the steps until I was securely inside the building. It felt as if I were moving in an alternate universe where I no longer had a love interest because my evil stepsister had stolen him away from me.

A lonely feeling plagued me when I entered my apartment. Suddenly, I remembered how little I had eaten at Court's party. It would've been wise of her to cross whoever catered dinner off her contacts list. The food was horrible at best. Still starving, I rushed to the kitchen and pulled open the refrigerator. I needed to eat, and it had to be something that could ease my despair, if only for a little while. I had all the fixings for a peanut butter and jelly sandwich, but as I stood in the chilly space between the door and the racks, I remembered the chocolate blast ice cream with large chunks of dark chocolate and Oreo cookies in the freezer. That would do.

I slammed the refrigerator door, opened the freezer, and found the full carton behind all the scallops, shrimp, and crab legs I wanted to cook but never had time for.

I tugged open the drawer where I kept my silverware and found a big spoon. It was as if my taste buds were in desperate need to have the flavors on my tongue. Plus, it was the fastest way to expunge Jake's delicious taste from my mouth. The ice cream was hard, but I managed to scoop out a hearty spoonful anyway and plop it into my mouth.

"Oh …" I said, warming the cold ice cream sitting on my tongue.

One spoonful after the next, and with each swallow, I thought less and less about Jake, or Asher, or whatever the hell he was calling himself at the moment.

Knock, knock, knock.

I stood up straight, spoon in my mouth, and my eyes grew wide. *Is it him? Has he come back to claim me?*

When I made it to the door, I saw that I'd forgotten to put down my spoon and pint of ice cream. I didn't want Jake, or Asher, to know I was gorging my blues away. "Dang it," I whispered.

"Who is it?" I called.

"It's me, Kit Kat," Zara said.

I was relieved but disappointed it wasn't Asher as well. I stuck my spoon into my softening ice cream and opened the door.

Zara, who was wearing sweaty shorts and a tank top, frowned at what was in my hands. "Oh my God. That bad, huh?"

I snorted. "Believe me, it was worse before this."

I invited her in, and for some odd reason, she turned on the light in the living room then turned it off.

"What are you doing?" I asked, frowning dubiously as I flopped down onto the sofa.

She sat carefully on the edge of the sofa beside me. "Nothing. I thought I wanted more light but decided I didn't." She waved her fingers toward me, asking for my dinner.

I sighed and handed her the carton. "Ice cream after a run, huh?"

She rolled her eyes.

"And what are you doing out running this late

anyway? You're begging to be dragged into the alley by creepy-rapist guy."

She held a large spoonful of my favorite ice cream in front of her mouth. "Or a creepy stalker gazing into the windows."

"What?" I asked, frowning.

"Nothing." She plopped the ice cream into her mouth then closed her eyes to relish the flavors. "Now, that's good." She gave the carton and spoon back to me.

Zara and I often ate from the same silverware and drank from the same cup. We were not queasy about sharing each other's germs. I always considered her my sister from another mother.

I snorted. "So, why did you leave the dinner? You left before we did."

She groaned, closing her eyes. "Long story, but it involves Kirk, the driver. I don't want to talk about it, not tonight."

"Wow, did you guys kiss?"

She looked at me with one eye open.

I shoved her playfully on the shoulder. "Oh my God, you did. Was it nice?"

"Personally, I think I should be the one asking the questions."

"Why do you say that?"

"Because you said the lovely Dr. Jake Sparrow has secrets. What are they?"

I sniffed, jerking my head back. "Come on. When have you known me to tell someone's secrets?"

Zara had a slight smirk on her face as she studied me. It was weird.

"What?" I asked then ran my tongue across my front teeth, wondering if I had chocolate on them or something.

"Nothing."

"Hey," I said, pointing my spoon at her. "You're the one who kissed Kirk. You're the one who has something to share, not me."

"Right," she said, rising to her feet, then she stretched while yawning. "I'm also the one who needs a shower. You smell lovely. Like man sweat and sex."

I laughed. She was right. I was drenched in Asher's scent.

"Plus, I have an early morning, and so do you." She held out her arms, and I stood to hug her.

"What are you doing tomorrow?" I asked.

Her eyes shone bright as she rubbed her hands together. "Photo shoot in Manhattan. Wish me luck."

"Luck," I said. "And wish me luck."

"Luck, because you're going to need it way more than I do," she said.

"Ha," I said as I showed her out.

Only after she left did I wonder why Zara presumed I would need more luck than her. Regardless, I was glad she was gone but only for one reason. I didn't want to share any more of my ice cream. I dropped back onto the sofa and continued eating it until it was all gone.

BLUE BUTTERFLY, YOUR WING'S CLIPPED. BLUE Butterfly, you're cruel. You shouldn't be so shaky. I shouldn't be a fool.

That was the chorus of the song. I silenced my alarm before it could repeat. The previous night before falling asleep, I'd eaten the entire pint of chocolate blast. Rich creaminess settled in my stomach like a log. Emotional gorging always had its consequences. A wave of nausea hit me, and while I closed my eyes, waiting for the sickness to pass, I tried to assess the emotional damage from the previous night's interaction with Jake or Asher. I groaned, clutching my belly, unable to focus on what I wanted to ponder.

When the nausea disappeared, I hopped to my feet, happy it was gone. I had no time to think about Asher, since I had to get ready to go to work. Once again, I found myself counting minutes as if they were Weight Watchers points.

First, I showered. That took eight minutes. Next, I pulled my hair back into a ponytail. That took less than a minute. I didn't take an extra minute to primp, even though I cared how I would look when I eventually ran into Asher. Frankly, I was too tired to fix any messes the mirror revealed.

Even though the sight of food made me want to hurl, I knew I had to pack snacks to keep my energy up throughout the day. It felt as though it had been forever since I prepared my nutrition for a long shift. I still had dry snacks in my bag, but once my belly was less cranky, I would be hungry enough to win a hot dog eating contest. Just about all my baby carrots had turned mushy and slimy, but I washed the freshest ones and put them in a plastic Ziploc bag. That took three minutes.

I was out of apples and oranges. *Note to self, go grocery shopping.* Then I remembered I should have a big bag of raw almonds in the cabinet. I padded over to the other side of the kitchen, found them in the cabinet, then put them in my bag as well.

Even though I felt as if I was leaving tons of things behind, it was time to go, so I grabbed my bag, rushed out of my apartment, went down the elevator, and once I stepped out of the building, my hopes were thwarted.

A part of me had expected to see Asher standing out front, waiting for me. Such a romantic gesture certainly wasn't beyond the realm of possibility. He had shown up at the airport yesterday, which impressed me. Then we'd walked to the bookstore and danced at the outdoor concert. All the flowers he left me every morning when I stayed at the penthouse, the masquerade party, the rides in hired cars—it all indicated that he was a romantic guy, but that morning, he wasn't.

Disappointed, I moved fast up the avenue, not paying much attention to those who were heading to the hospital to start their shifts with me. I had to put my mind into surgeon mode. A long time had passed since I'd gone more than two days without being in the OR. Strangely, I hadn't missed it much. I might have had senioritis as far as my residency was concerned. It was almost over, and I needed a bigger break than two days. I needed frivolous time to do nothing but sleep in for several days and not worry about my missing mother or how a patient was progressing throughout his recovery.

I wanted to read a newspaper and learn who was who in the world. *What about those Blackstones?* Asher had two brothers and a sister. Never had I been more curious about them than I was then.

Freedom was on the horizon, but when I stepped onto the grassy quad of the hospital grounds, I stretched my fingers. I hoped I was scheduled to perform an early procedure. An early surgery was just what I needed to put me solidly back in a surgeon's state of mind.

"Morning, Pen," Kevin said as he swept past me just before I entered the lobby.

He didn't even give me time to respond, which was odd because he wasn't the type to not wait for me to say good morning back.

When I entered the building, Cecily and Nina, the two check-in clerks, observed me without saying a thing.

"Good morning, ladies," I said since they wouldn't.

They both looked down at the desk, as if something had suddenly occupied their attention. That was weird.

I passed two other familiar faces walking toward the care station, and they averted their eyes too.

I chewed on my lower lip. Right. Not only had Asher and I left the party early, but we'd made it clear we were a couple. They didn't know that Julia Valentine had tossed a grenade into our hot and heavy love affair the previous night. As far as they knew, Asher and I were blissfully breaking the rules.

But I wanted to yell at everybody to give me a break. I was almost done. Like, I literally had my big toe on the finish line.

The care station was in sight, and Deb was standing at the counter, doing paperwork. I'd forgotten about the look on her face when she got an up-close-and-personal view of Asher and me kissing. *Damn it.*

"Penina, let's talk," Deb said without looking up from her paperwork once I made it to an EMR station.

Panic made me feel as if I had been struck with a sudden bout of vertigo. "Talk about what?"

She swooped up the papers and file folders off the counter. "A lot. Follow me."

We went into one of the small instruction rooms off the central care station. Her expression was unreadable, but she watched me closely as I sat across from her at the table.

"How involved with an attending are you?" she finally asked.

Yes, it was slight hostility in her eyes. I wanted to make some smart-ass comment, asking her how involved we looked. I sure as hell wasn't going to let myself be written up for falling in love with Jake Sparrow, not then or ever.

"Deb, I'm less than a month away from being a fellow. So just let it go."

She stabbed the tabletop. "But you're still a resident now, and I'm still your supervisor."

"So what are you asking? You want me to lay off of—" *What do I call him?* The previous night, before I'd gotten out of the limo, he said everyone should get used to calling him Asher. But it was his duty to inform our colleagues first, not mine.

Deb watched me curiously. "Dr. Sparrow," she said, finishing for me. "Are you okay, Penina? It's been a while since you've been on shift, and you look very tired."

I sat up straight, attempting to appear as though I had more energy. Deb's perception was spot-on. I was tired, more emotionally than physically. "I'm fine."

"Well," she said with a sigh, "you and Dr. Sparrow are adults. I wish you would've said something. I didn't enjoy finding out that way."

I nodded. "I understand. I'm sorry."

"Apology accepted." She opened a folder. "But I asked you here for a different reason. You have a fellowship offer from this hospital and—"

Claudette, one of the triage nurses, pushed the door open wide and announced, "Deb, we have reporters all over the place."

———

It had gotten out and spread like wildfire. All media outlets, big and small, print and internet, reported Asher Blackstone was a neurosurgeon at Unity Medical Center in New Orleans, Louisiana.

I'd never known how vastly popular the Blackstones were. As I stood at the EMR machine, searching for my assigned patients, everyone around me talked about Asher, their voices spiked with excitement. It was as if people had just found out Prince William had gone missing for six years and turned up in New Orleans.

"When did you learn who he was, Penina?" Angela asked during handoffs.

I stopped searching the database and looked at all the curious faces watching me. I shrugged. "A few days ago."

"Then the last time we saw each other, you didn't know?"

My cold glare didn't seem to faze her. She still appeared insistent that I answer.

"No," I muttered, not because I didn't want to upset her but because it was the truth. I sighed sharply. "And where are my handoffs?"

"You're off rotation," Angela said.

With one hand on my hip and the other massaging my right temple, I closed my eyes, needing a moment to process that. How could a surgeon, especially one of my caliber, be off rotation? Was Deb punishing me for last night?

"What?" I finally asked.

Angela raised her eyebrows as she shrugged. That was her way of saying, "Tough luck, and that's what you get for screwing around with Asher Blackstone."

I stomped away from the EMR console, on my way to find Deb and have it out with her. I was plodding down the corridor where all the patient care consult rooms were when a large hand covered my mouth and an even stronger arm wrapped around my waist, and someone carried me off.

At first, I was shocked, then I became terrified as I realized I couldn't yell for help, bite, or elbow the guy. And I only thought to use my heel to kick him in the shin when he had already pulled me into one of the lightless exam rooms.

"Dr. Ross," he whispered, his mouth close to my ear. "Don't scream. It's me."

"Who?" I asked, although I couldn't do more than hum the word.

"Me, Greg Carroll." He removed his hand.

"Greg Carroll?"

"Yes. I'm going to turn on the light."

I shook like a leaf, but at least I felt less afraid as the light clicked on and it was indeed him.

Nine

ASHER BLACKSTONE

12 HOURS AGO

From where I sat in the back of the limo, I could see Penina standing in front of the elevator. I kept my focus glued to the entrance of the building, making sure no one sketchy came in behind her. My eyes narrowed a fraction more as I paid attention to how delicate she looked with her arms folded tightly against her ribs and her shoulders hunched. Then I pictured her erect nipples against my tongue and the heated flesh of her breast in my mouth. It took every ounce of willpower to stay put.

I was less of a man and more of a deadbeat boyfriend for not at least escorting her to her apartment. But I knew why I couldn't do that. I wanted a lot during my lifetime, but never had I wanted anything more than to make love to Penina that night.

I had no surgeries scheduled for the next day. Penina thought her shift started at five a.m. But it had been decided. Her residency was complete. In the morning, when her alarm played the song about the blue butterfly, I was going to reveal that Si would be presenting her with a fellowship she couldn't refuse. Then I would draw her under me, separating her thighs, and ram my engorged cock into her wet wonderland. Later, when we were done making love, we would go to the hospital, and sign the contract, and wouldn't have to report back to the hospital until the first of October. For several months, Penina Ross would be all mine.

I was the boss. I was in charge. And I had securely ensured that surgical duties wouldn't hinder me indulging in Penina Ross. The only obstacle that could get in the way of my need to overdose on her had sent several text messages to my cell phone and then had the balls to call. When Julia wanted something, she sought to acquire it with all guns blazing. She was capable of anything and was an expert at pulling the rug right out from under a person's feet while looking them in the eye.

I pressed the button on the console to talk to Kirk. We were still separated by a tinted window. I would've rolled it down, but I wanted to keep the sweet aroma of Penina's skin, which filled the air, all to myself.

"Ready," I said.

He started the engine and pulled away from the curb.

I was restless in my seat, unable to get comfortable. Asher Blackstone was back and residing beneath my skin. I wanted Penina to read the book about my family, which had some true details about me, and decide whether she could love me or not. Jake was a man with no past or future. He existed in that beautiful reality called the present. In the present, I had made love to Penina, taken her dancing, and bared my soul to her. Jake carried no shame, nor was he burdened with constantly feeling inadequate.

I wiped my hands over my face and sighed wearily into my palms.

My feet were back on the chessboard. Julia was a parasite threatening my tranquility. I had to make moves that ensured I wouldn't get eaten up from the inside out or lose the one woman I'd ever loved. That was why as Asher Blackstone, I picked up my cell phone and made a call.

I DROPPED MY PHONE ON THE SEAT THEN GRIMACED while shaking my fists. I was agitated. The call I'd made to my sister, Bryn, had gone straight to voice mail. I was losing both my sanity and my resolve.

How did Julia know how to find me, anyway? It couldn't have been Spencer. He wasn't the same brother I could never trust. I shook my head. It wasn't him. And it sure as hell wasn't Jasper.

"Ash?" Kirk's voice rang through the speakers as the culprit's face came to mind.

I stretched my neck, hot under the collar as I smashed the communication button. "Yeah, Kirk?"

"I see reporters in front of your building. A whole lot of them."

They knew where to find me, which further supported my conclusion that it was Gina who'd sold me out. However, it wasn't her style to throw the press a bone. That was all Julia.

"How far away are we?"

"They're watching my approach."

"Should I make a U-turn?" he asked.

"No. That'll only alert them. Don't slow down, but don't speed up. Cruise past at the speed limit."

"Got it."

The action was performed to perfection. A few of the reporters looked after the limo as if something of value might be inside, but none of them followed up on their suspicions.

"It worked," Kirk said. "Where to now?"

I glared out the window as we passed storefronts of closed businesses. New Orleans wasn't my home. If we were in New York or Rhode Island, I would have plenty of places to hide. But there, I was a sitting duck. I couldn't go to the hospital either. The most sagacious reporters would be camped out there, pretending to be patients. But none of them were loitering in front of the place I had just left.

"Damn," I said under my breath.

Penina and I would have to sleep in the same building tonight.

I ASKED KIRK TO LET ME OUT IN FRONT OF THE Popeye's chicken place on Canal Street. The sun was down, but the night was still as muggy as hell as

I walked up the avenue. It was late, but a lot of rabble-rousers were still out, stumbling out of the French Quarter, intoxicated and searching for their next bit of excitement.

Sweat rolled down my back and covered my skin when I made it to the boarding hold. Even though air conditioning would've been nice, I had to stand out in the humidity a while longer to make sure the coast was clear. I kept out of sight under an awning of Barba's Salon across the street.

My attention kept veering toward Penina's apartment on the third floor. The one Si had given me the keys to was on the opposite side of the building and a floor up. The distance between our apartments would help me battle my craving for her, but still, it would be hard getting through the night without knocking on her door. I doubted I would be able to do it.

"Jake, is that you?" a woman with an English accent asked.

I flinched and turned to see a pretty raven-haired woman who very much resembled one of my surgical mentees jogging in my direction.

"Zara? Are you out jogging at this hour?"

"Yeah," she said as if my concern didn't faze her.

"It's pretty late for that, don't you think?"

She pressed her hands onto her hips then bent over to catch her breath. "I'm running because I needed the exercise to clear my head." She made a high-pitched sound when she sighed. "Although it's as humid as hell out here. What the hell was I thinking?"

"Are you okay? Do you need water?"

She raised a hand as she dragged herself up to stand tall. "I'll be fine. But what are you doing standing in the dark? Are you spying on Pen?"

"No, but you're aware of how dangerous it is for a woman to be out this late jogging alone, don't you?"

She pressed her hand onto the brick wall next to me and hiked up one of her legs to stretch it. "Okay, Mr. Money Bags, you're not my father or my man, so cool the concern." Her eyebrows fluttered upward twice. "I'm also self-defense certified."

"You're right. I'll cool the concern, especially since you're self-defense certified."

She stretched her other leg. "That's right, and you never answered my question. Are you stalking Penina?"

"No."

"Then what are you doing out here in the

dark?"

"I live here."

"The hell you do."

"Yes, I do. But don't tell anybody."

"Why not?" she countered. "You have secrets up to here, Jake Sparrow. And you have my friend keeping them for you. It's driving her bonkers, but I'm not keeping your secrets."

I wanted to laugh at her. I could see why she and Penina were so close. They both had bold and honest traits about them.

"I understand. Listen, I'll tell you what she knows about me if you don't rat me out."

She shook her head as if my words stung her. "Rat you out to who exactly?"

"The whole world?"

"Ha," she scoffed as she transitioned to extend one arm across her body and reached over to grab her shoulder. "Is your ego really that large?"

I took a step closer and made sure we had good eye contact and said, "My name is Asher Blackstone. You know, the Blackstone family."

Her arms fell to her sides as she gasped and leaned back so fast that I thought she would tip over. "No way. You're the missing one. The one they say murdered his father."

I rolled my eyes as I shook my head emphatically. *Who the started that rumor, anyway?* "I didn't murder my father."

She folded her arms. "That's not what they say. They say they have proof. And the fact that you've gone frolicking through the world, pretending to be Jake Sparrow, doesn't make you look innocent. Nice fake name, though."

I opened my mouth to set her mind at ease about me being a murderer and reveal what only my family members, Gina, and Penina knew, but she said, "So, Penina is shagging a Blackstone? Talk about jackpot. She's rich."

I couldn't help but toss my head back and laugh.

"All hell's about to break loose, isn't it?" she asked.

I took a deep breath and nodded. "But hey, could you do me a favor? Could you check on her and make sure she made it to her apartment safely? I dropped her off after we left the party."

"And you didn't stay with her?"

I shook my head, gazing up at the window. Her warm and soft body was probably between her sheets. She often slept nude. I recalled how her round ass felt against me.

"Then you are stalking her," Zara said as if she had caught me in a lie.

I ripped my gaze away from her window. "I'm not stalking Penina. I told you—I live here. I'm going up in a few. The press knows I'm in town. I want to make sure no one's hiding out, waiting to pounce."

She regarded me shrewdly. "Well, I'm not telling."

I sighed with relief. "Thank you. I appreciate it."

Zara smirked. "You're welcome, Dr. Blackstone, and to really put your mind at ease, I'll turn her light on and off when I'm inside her flat." She winked.

I figured it was time to reveal something else to her. "Thank you, Zara. You're a good friend to a beautiful woman whom I love."

I saw that my words had the intended effect when her lips formed an O as her eyes grew wide. "Oh, in love, are we? You haven't known each other more than a month." Then she raised a hand. "Forget what I said. It's Penina. If I were a man or a lesbian, I'd, as you Americans say, book her ass too."

She made me laugh again, and I liked it. I

wondered what Sanjay would think to know his beautiful, foul-mouthed daughter who was brave enough to run in the city at night had dropped out of the residency program at the last minute. There was no way he was going to hear it from me, but he wouldn't like what she had done. That was for sure. He'd mentioned his brilliant daughter at least twice in every conversation I ever had with him. As far as he was concerned, she was the only woman that should be cutting open a brain.

I watched Penina's window until the light turned on then off.

"Well done, Zara," I whispered then crossed the street.

THE BOARDING-HOLD APARTMENT WASN'T AS DISMAL as I remembered it. The furniture was sleek and modern, and so were the appliances. All of it probably cost less than my shoes. I wasn't bragging about that. Instead, I thought, maybe I should pay attention to how much money I spend on frivolous crap. Truth be told, Jake Sparrow went through money just as fast as Asher Blackstone had.

I was sitting on the edge of the sofa, not ready

to get comfortable yet, when I received a text from Bryn. My body stiffened when I read, *Ash, I'm in New Orleans and ready to see you. Where are you?*

My gaze darted around the room. The air around me stood still, like the calm before a raging storm. My twin sister was a car ride away. I couldn't wait to see her, but I also dreaded her arrival. But I needed her. She had taken Julia on before and won. Plus, Bryn never lost a skirmish. She was the sort of firepower I needed to put Julia away.

"Carter Valentine," I whispered.

That was Julia's brother. I wondered why I was suddenly thinking about him. A memory crept into my mind.

CARTER AND I ARE BOYS IN A MUSTY ROOM THAT *smells of cigars and perfume, the sweet kind young girls wear. The walls are red leather. His father, Arthur, stone-faced, red lines streaking through the whites of his eye, brows furrowed, as always, shoves Carter toward bare hips and pubic hair. That's all I can remember about her—the girl's genitals. Carter cowers against the wall, hugging his legs as he buries his face in his knees.*

"No, Father. No!" he cries.

"I got no use for a boy like you. No use," Arthur says

from somewhere in the room. I can't see him. I don't want to see him.

"Get them out of here, pansies," my father says.

I'm being pushed. My legs are trying to keep up with the force of the thrust. Then I'm out of the room.

THAT MEMORY HAD BEEN BURIED SOMEWHERE DEEP inside me until then. No wonder Carter hated vagina, although I couldn't say if he replaced his disdain for the female anatomy with a lust for his own. I always thought of him as asexual, preferring not to engage in the messy business of sexual intercourse. I came to that conclusion because when we were kids, he occasionally visited the mansion during the summers. He often joined Spencer and me when we went swimming in the sound. Spence and I would drop our trousers on the beach and change into our trunks. Carter would freeze, turn away from us, and beg us to let him know when we were covered "down there." He had other quirks, too, like holding his piss until he almost urinated on himself because he didn't like to whip his cock out and touch it.

But the memory … *What would I have done if it were me being pushed toward the sexual organs of a pubes-*

cent girl? I wouldn't have had sex with her, that's for certain. My father must've known that, which was why he was the one who'd put an end to the charade, saving himself from the same kind of embarrassment Valentine had suffered by his son's reaction. Carter's cowering had won me my escape. We weren't the only ones traumatized by what happened either. The girl's thighs, which looked like flagpoles, trembled like two reeds in the wind. Why had it taken so long for my father to die? If life was fair, he would've given up the ghost right then and there.

I rubbed the back of my neck as I shot to my feet, but then sat back down just as fast. I didn't want to remember that. I wished I hadn't.

Julia was aware of Carter's demons, bred by incidents like the ones I recalled, and how they haunted him all the way up until adulthood. He was as scared as hell of his father, Arthur Valentine. All she had to do was threaten to squeal on him, since Arthur reviled his son enough to always take her side, and Carter would do whatever she told him to do. She wanted to know more about my brothers and me, so she'd had him put cameras in our bedrooms.

Julia was more deceitful than intelligent. She

wasn't blessed with the capability to think things through. Since her cameras were wireless, their signals interfered with our surveillance systems, which were part of the daily monitoring of the estate. When Jasper found out, he pulled the recordings, which showed Carter putting the finishing touches on the cameras before tiptoeing out of the bedrooms.

As a child, Carter had been forced to hang with the boys, but when he got older, he preferred to keep Bryn company. That was why Jasper showed her the video first. Bryn swore that if Carter had done something like that, then Julia put him up to it. Regardless, Jasper banned him from the estate and threatened to take the incident to Father and Valentine.

Bryn asked if she could do something first—a plan to help Carter. After a lot of begging, Jasper acquiesced. Bryn was able to convince Carter to perform the impossible. In each bedroom, in front of every camera, the two of them crawled under the covers naked and pretended to have sex. He touched breasts, rubbed thighs, and everything. Bryn told me that he puked his guts out after each session.

At first, the result worked in Carter's favor. His

father no longer questioned his sexuality, and he was still banned from the Blackstone mansion, a place he hated. But a year before my father's death, he and Valentine came up with a scheme to have Carter and Bryn marry each other. None of us knew it then, but that decision was the beginning of the end of the Blackstones and the Valentines as we knew ourselves.

So Bryn had an expert's aptitude for scheming, and that was why I wanted to seek her advice about how to get rid of Julia for good.

ARE YOU BEING FOLLOWED? I REPLIED.

I DON'T THINK SO. WHY?

JULIA ALERTED THE MEDIA TO MY WHEREABOUTS AND possibly more.

AFTER SEVERAL MINUTES, SHE WROTE BACK, *COME see me here,* and she added an address.

Ten

ASHER BLACKSTONE

I took a cab to a modest house in Metairie next to a cemetery. When the car exited the offramp, I asked the driver how long we had before arrival.

"Not long, a matter of minutes," he said in his lyrical New Orleans accent.

I called Bryn and told her I was close. When I arrived, she stood from sitting in a swinging bench on the porch and held up a bottle of bourbon and two whisky glasses. We stood smirking at each other, as we usually did when we hadn't seen each other in a long time. Bryn and I had a way of conveying emotions to each other, a connection shared by those who escaped the womb on the same day and around the same time.

"Is that a cemetery behind the house?"

She sniffed. "Really? With all the demons haunting the place we grew up in, you're scared of a horde of pissed-off Southern ghosts?"

I chortled as I made my approach. "Not in the least."

"Plus, no one's going to be looking for you out here."

She had already set the bourbon and glasses down on a small round table, which freed her up to jump on me when I was close enough.

"Oh my God, Ash, don't ever do that again!"

She kissed me multiple times on my cheek before releasing me.

"I won't," I said then gave her an up close once-over. She had on a pair of loose-fitting jeans and a white tank top. I was used to seeing her bones poke at her skin, but she had put on an attractive layer of weight. "You look good, Bryn—healthy."

Her smile grew bigger and her eyes more excited. "I know. I've been happy, Ash," she said, nodding. "Really happy."

"You look it."

She looked me up and down. "And you look good, too, and snazzy. Did you have a date tonight?"

"I went to a party."

Her eyebrows flitted up and stayed there. "Oh, was it fun?"

I could feel myself inside Penina while we were in the back of the limousine, and I thought of her soft, warm body, then I licked my bottom lip, remembering the taste of her tongue. "Up until a point."

"Was your night ruined by Julia?"

I pressed my lips together, nodding.

We stared at each other, grinning. The fact that she was right there in front of me felt incredible. God, I missed the hell out of her.

"Well, come, have a seat. Let's start with some butterscotch bourbon."

"Ha," I scoffed. "I see you haven't changed in that department." She couldn't just drink straight-up liquor without there being an added flavor. I appreciated remembering that minor detail about my sister. It made me feel close to her again.

"A lot has changed about me, but not being able to drink bourbon straight hasn't."

We laughed as we settled on the bench. She poured two glasses of liquor, handed me one, then kept one for herself.

"So, Ash, why did you run away?" she asked.

I drew in a deep breath through my nose. "You're not wasting any time, are you?"

She shook her head. "I have no time to waste. You're going to have to get back to the city pretty soon and handle Julia."

I leaned away from her, frowning. "What are you saying?"

Bryn patted me on the thigh then circled two fingers in front of me. "Your energy is neurotic, and you're trembling. I'm guessing your state of mind has a lot to do with Julia because she knows how to get to you." She tilted her head to study my perplexed expression. "You know you're very much like Carter. And that's why she knows how to push your buttons, *and* that's why you want to run away from her."

I sniffed and took a drink of bourbon as she kept her narrowed eyes on me. There was no use in defending myself against her likening me to Carter. I was nothing like that guy as far as I was concerned, but she certainly had the right to her belief.

"You really look good, too, though," she said finally. "Tired and weird with the dark hair but still very handsome and healthy."

I ran a hand through my hair as I took another

swig of my drink then set it on the table. "So you're not going to help me with Julia?"

She smiled graciously as she shook her head. "No. You're going to have to deal with her yourself. I'm not getting involved." She patted me on the back. "But you can handle the likes of Julia. You're smarter than she is, and you have more integrity. You can battle her and win."

That generous smile was on her face again.

"Why are you looking at me that way?" she asked.

I rubbed my mouth to scrub away the frown. "What happened to you? Why have you changed so much?"

She tilted her head curiously. "Disappointed?"

"No. Not at all."

Bryn held her glass to her lips. "It's a long story." She took a drink then squeezed her eyes shut, as she always did when she drank liquor.

"Well, I've got nothing but time."

"No, you don't." She winked. "And it's a story that, instead of repeating, bears forgetting."

"I doubt that," I said, smiling at her.

She took another drink and the strength of the liquor made her cough. "You're not sleeping, are you?" Her voice was strained.

"How'd you know?"

"We're triplets. I know every phase of your face."

I grunted. "Triplets. I've been trying to forget that. How is she, anyway?"

She patted my thigh again as her eyes danced. "You know what's so funny?"

"What?" I didn't sound amused or as happy as she was. I figured whatever she had to say had to do with our real mother and the extra sister we'd discovered we had.

"Kat thought she saw you in Sydney three years ago. You were on a special surgical unit tasked to operate on some diplomat from Eastern Europe. I told her that man couldn't possibly be you because I didn't know you ever had an interest in pursuing medicine, let alone neurosurgery. How did you keep that from me?"

The truth was the first thing that came to my mind, which was why I shifted abruptly, causing the swing to creak.

"Spit it out, Ash. I can handle it. I'm a big girl now."

I watched her with a lopsided smile. "You sure are." And I was a big boy. "My interest in medicine belonged to me. I thought if I hid it, no one could take it away from me, not even you."

She pressed her lips together as she nodded. I'd hurt her feelings, and to console her, I rubbed her thigh just as she had done.

"It's okay," she said, choked up, then cleared her throat. "I know I used to be a bitch. We used to do things to hurt and control each other because we had no control over ourselves. We were taught to be that way." She sat her petite hand on top of mine. "And I'm glad you went out on your hero's journey. You're successful, and I heard you were in love too."

I wasn't surprised Spencer couldn't keep my relationship with Penina to himself.

"I am," I confessed. "What about you? Are you still with Dale?"

"No way. Dale is still chasing tail, cocaine, and pipe dreams."

"Then you dumped him?"

She sighed. "A long time ago."

I was waiting for Bryn to ridicule him some more but instead she recounted tales about her recent travels and the people she met along the way. She was about to hop on a flight to Marrakesh when she got the phone call from Spencer about me.

"But I've stayed in tents the size of a compact car. And the best thing I've ever done was the glass igloo in Kakslauttanen, Finland, falling asleep under the aurora borealis. It was so damn surreal. I never felt so—" She stared thoughtfully at the cemetery across the street. "So here. In existence in God's great big beautiful world. And I would've never seen or experienced any of it if I hadn't found the courage to finally leave Dale in my dust."

The way the light caught Bryn's silvery skin and delicate pink mouth made her appear transformed into an angelic being. *Who is this person? What has the angel sitting beside me done to my devilish and neurotic sister?* I didn't miss the old her, but I wished she hadn't had to be away from me to find that new version of herself.

I watched her face turn brighter as she spoke about the pyramids of Giza and how humbling it was to stand on ancient ground. After Marrakesh, she planned to return to Thailand to join a group of seniors she'd met in Singapore on an ocean-exploration expedition.

I had nearly finished my second glass of bourbon. My head was light, and that meant I'd had enough, although I hadn't been that relaxed in a while. I sniffed, chuckling as I put my glass on the table. "Hanging with the wise bunch, huh?"

Bryn set her glass next to mine. "All five of them are retired archeologists, and I was so lucky ..." Bryn furrowed her eyebrows then quickly scooted back against the bench and shook her head. "I'm talking too much."

"No, it's okay. I like listening."

"Well, I don't like talking too much about myself. I'm working on ego-speaking. I want to hear about other people more than indulge in myself."

"It's okay to indulge in yourself when you're interesting. And you have become interesting as hell."

She smiled graciously as her gaze danced around my face. "I can hardly believe I'm sitting here talking to you, Ash. I missed you so much." She touched her chest and sniffed. "Just ..." She closed her eyes and sighed. "Don't ever leave me again, okay?"

I gently caressed her face. "I won't."

"You'd better not. So ..." She rubbed her hands together and clapped the tips of her fingers twice. "Tell me about your girl. I bet she's lovely."

I told her how intelligent my girl was and

admitted that it was her beautiful face that inspired me the most.

"There's something about the way her features are placed. It's like she's art made specifically for me. I know it sounds superficial."

"No," she said quickly. "Not at all. She was made for you, and you were able to look at her and tell." She rubbed her hands together. "I want to meet her. When can I meet her?"

I yawned hard. "Damn it," I said, shaking my head briskly. "Sorry about that."

"It's okay. You're tired. Why don't you just go upstairs and go to bed?"

The motionless, warm, and wet night, the trees, opaque in the dark like hairy cavemen, the bourbon, Bryn, our conversation—it all made my eyelids heavier than usual.

After standing, I stretched my body from side to side and yawned again. "I think I should."

Bryn raised her arms above her head to stretch. "It's a beautiful night, isn't it?"

I focused on the chair swing tied to a thick branch on the oak tree. "Yeah." I sighed, thinking about how nice it would be if Penina were here.

"Ash?" she called quietly.

I turned to look at her.

"Although I won't get involved in your Julia Valentine predicament, I do have some advice for you. Do you want to hear it?"

Bryn had tilted her head as she waited for my reply. As long as I'd known her, which was all my life, she'd never done that—asked before issuing advice.

"Sure," I said.

"Be nice to her. That's how you're going to send Julia packing. You've always treated her like crap and vice versa. Julia, unfortunately, is burdened by untreated abusive-daddy issues."

My grimace intensified while I tried to make the connections in my brain. "Okay."

"Think about it. Remember we used to call her dad AV Dingleberry?"

I snorted a chuckle and nodded.

"For this purpose, and since we are practicing being real mature adults, let's take the Dingleberry part off and call him AV."

"What the hell happened to you? Has an alien invaded your body?"

She chuckled. "I'm standing right here."

"Don't get me wrong. I'm not complaining, but please ..." I folded my arms. "Continue."

"Well, AV purported to love Julia, but look what

his love entailed. Remember how he used to parade her in front of guests at parties and say how sexy she was and how she was going to be a real asset? Even forcing her to marry Jasper when she liked you more. She's as scared as hell of Jasper. Being treated like crap is Julia's comfortable place, and when you treat her that way, she wants more of you. Talk to her, be nice, and I bet she'll go somewhere else and find another poor soul who makes her feel like AV does."

I nodded and said, "Okay."

As we hugged good night, Bryn's words wouldn't leave me. *Did I treat Julia like crap?* It had been a long time since I'd interacted with her. I had to think hard to recall our encounters.

The room upstairs was as quaint and modest as the rest of the house. The space looked like something straight out of a horror movie, though. Sheer white curtains covered the windows. The material was so flimsy, they may as well not have been there. There were two twin beds, one on each side of the room, and a stuffed animal sitting on a rocking chair. *How did Bryn find this place?*

I took off my pants, button-down shirt, T-shirt, and socks, folded each, and sat them on the rocking chair. Then I turned off the light and stretched out across the small bed. When I lifted my head, I saw that my feet were dangling over the edge. I'd never been that uncomfortable in a bed before, not even in a call room. But it didn't matter. Bryn and I were in the same house again.

I stared at the ceiling, wanting to give in to sleep but also fight it while striving to picture Julia's face. The act was like focusing on an eye chart and trying to read the bottom line. Her face and body were a blur, although her personality and the crazy stuff she used to do were as clear as the top line of that same chart.

Our last interaction had taken place at a private island on the Hudson River. I invited her to a friend of a friend of a friend's party. Julia had arrived before me, which was something she always did. It was a tactic. The early bird got the advantage of reading the room, knowing the players, and disarming the late birds.

She had already started with a guy named Rudy Lawson, a financier out of Manhattan. He was high on cocaine. She was not. Julia knew how to stay sober, which was another choice she made to garner an advantage over the drug-addicted rich people we often hung around.

Rudy was all over her with octopus hands, and

she let him rub her thighs and slide his fingers up and down her slit while he tongued her. No one cared that they were a few strokes and gropes removed from getting it on while in public. That was the sort of craziness that went on at parties on private islands. Regardless, Julia was always aware when I walked into the room. She wanted me to see what she was doing. Her goal was to provoke me— make me feel jealous and worthless.

I homed in on him kissing and sucking on her neck, his mouth making its way to her fake tits. I was mad as hell. The thing was that she never had a reaction to sexual stimulation, not even while I was doing it. Her body was an object, a means to an end. And even though I knew that, it didn't stop me from wanting to rip Rudy's head off.

Suddenly, I recalled a woman approaching me while I remained zeroed in on Julia. When I looked at her, it was as if she wasn't there. I imagined she introduced herself and said something about knowing who I was and being glad to finally meet me. My heart would've been racing like a gazelle narrowly escaping the jaws of a predator. I would've been driven mad by the blatant disrespect.

My memory of that night on the private island was interrupted by one of Penina sitting next to

Greg Carroll at Nurse Peters's party. He'd felt the good vibes that being next to her aroused and was drunk on them, wanting them all for himself. When she saw me, she smiled, though, warm and reassuring. Even though I hated that he was drinking up the attention that should've been mine, in the end, she was mine, and Penina would do nothing to jeopardize what was happening between us.

Julia, though—she didn't do that. She guided her hips more toward Rudy's finger-banging and tongued the guy harder and deeper while eyeing me the whole time.

"Why didn't you leave?" I whispered to the dark room.

Why did I storm in her direction, jerk her off Lawson's lap, and drag her away, searching from room to room until I found one that had a leather couch? The piece of furniture I shoved her down on was brown, shiny, and hard, and when she hit the cushion, she slammed against it. I knew it hurt her, and that got me hard. I hated hurting women but not Julia. I took a condom out of my pocket—I knew to never enter her without one—and put the rubber on, grabbed Julia by her hips, and slammed myself inside her. I wanted it to hurt.

Julia laughed as I banged her. "Harder, you loser. Harder you weak man!" she kept shouting.

That memory ...

Rubbing my eyes, I remembered the next part. I *had* done her harder. She stopped insulting and started crying out with pleasure. And still, I wanted to burst through her and destroy her. But the next move in our charade belonged to me. One hard thrust, then I pulled out of her, stuffed my unspent cock back into my pants, and zipped and buttoned them. I glared at her. She breathed heavily. Then she licked a finger, soaking it with saliva, and then slid it in and out of her wetness, trying to tempt me into finishing inside her. Julia needed that. It was her power. She knew how difficult it was to get me to come with her. It was all about control. I wanted to blow my load inside her, but then I would've lost. And to ensure my victory, I turned away from her and calmly walked out of the room.

I had sex with someone else shortly thereafter, though I didn't know who she was. I had to finish what Julia started, and any woman would do. I was an animal, a moron. But not anymore.

That was customary in my relationship with Julia. She disrespected me, and I did the same by withholding sex, refusing to ejaculate, or stopping before she came. And that meant that Bryn's advice was spot-on. I had treated Julia like dirt.

"Damn." I rubbed my eyes harder. I'd never been so tired as I turned on my side.

I took solace in the fact that I wasn't that guy anymore. *But could Julia bring him back to the surface? Could she make me hurt Penina so severely that I lost the only woman I'd ever fallen in love with?* I feared that she could, and that was why I tried to make myself comfortable in that kid's bed and not between Penina's thighs.

Eleven

PENINA ROSS

"**W**hat is wrong with you?" I shouted at Greg.

His finger flew to his lips as he said, "Shush. If the team gets wind that I'm here, they'll put a stop to what I'm trying do."

I breathed heavily, like a mad bull staring down a red cape, as I observed him. His skin was blotchy and pale.

"Just, uh ..." Greg searched around him, turning in circles, until he moved to a chair and plopped down in it.

My anger transformed into concern. "Are you okay?" I asked, approaching him. I pressed the back of my hand against his forehead.

"You smell good," he whispered, eyes closed.

I narrowed my eyes at his euphoric expression, reminding myself that he probably wasn't in his right mind. Usually, patients made unintended statements when their brains were out of sorts.

"You're burning up," I said.

"This morning, I brushed my teeth, shaved, and showered. I can't remember the order, but before I could grab something to eat, I'd forgotten how I got home last night. Then I looked at myself in the mirror and couldn't remember who I was. I just sat down, waiting for it to pass, and it did. After that, I came straight here. I need you to find out what's wrong with me. I'm at the end of my rope." He said all of that in a rush. The good news was that I was able to keep up.

"Well, let's get you down to imaging—"

His hand flew up to cradle my waist. "No. No imaging. No one can see me."

"Well, someone has to do it, and it can't be me because I don't know how to work the equipment."

"Don't you have someone who's loyal to you? What about Sparrow?"

I gazed off. *What about Sparrow?* That was a good question. "He's not in today."

"Is there someone else?"

I twisted my mouth as I pondered his question. "Perhaps there is. Stay put."

Greg nodded. "I will."

Before I could turn away, he clamped his other hand down on my waist to stop me from going.

"I'm sorry for scaring you like that. You're the only one I can trust."

Gosh, he looked so vulnerable and so in need of my help. "It's over." I scrunched one side of my face. "But try another way to get my attention next time. That was scary as hell. I think I'm going to have to sign up for my friend's self-defense course after that."

He chuckled but didn't let go of me. "Another thing," he said.

I straightened my posture, putting my serious-doctor mask back on. "Yes?"

"I have a crush on you. I always have. Since I first saw you at Heathcliff's trade party."

I stepped out of his gentle grasp. "I'm taken, so the nature of our——"

"But you're not married." He smirked mischievously.

As a thought came to me, I folded my arms. "You're not faking your symptoms to get next to me, are you?"

His hands flew up to show me his palms. "No. That's not what this is about. I figured full disclosure was in order."

"Humph." I studied him with one eye narrowed. It was hard to determine whether I should believe him or not. I would have to wait for the scans to tell me the truth. His symptoms were severe. If they were real, the brain scan would show the damage.

I sighed. "Just wait here. Lock the door. You have my number. Call me if someone tries to open it."

His flirtatious grin came back. "I'll call you if someone doesn't."

I shook my head continuously. "You're making me doubt there's something wrong with you."

Greg chuckled. "That was a joke, Dr. Ross. I do that when I'm scared. It's how I lighten the mood."

"Well, then, don't do that. If this is serious, then behave as though it's serious."

"Damn," he whispered, watching me as if he was dazed. Then he took in a deep breath. "Okay. I will."

I rolled my eyes but still turned and walked out of the room. As soon as I could, I planned to hand off Greg's case. There were only three people I could trust to keep Greg's condition private. Asher wasn't around, and Angela didn't have the pull to keep imaging and the lab from blabbing to the whole hospital that Greg Carroll was in the facility.

I stood in front of the third person's office. After taking a deep breath, I braced myself and knocked.

"COME IN," CHIEF BROWN SAID.

I slowly opened the door, and when the chief saw me, his face lit up.

"Dr. Ross. Are you here about the offer?"

I couldn't stop my mouth from cracking a smirk. *Are we really going to pretend that my new boyfriend isn't his best friend and that I knew he knew all along that Jake Sparrow is Asher Blackstone?*

I took the necessary time to fold my arms across my chest, doing it slowly and confidently. "Did Asher put you up to it? Since he owns the hospital?"

His happy expression dropped. "I see."

I let my arms fall to my sides. Acting like a bitch wasn't my style. I really wished I had done that differently.

"Sorry about that," I said, shaking my head. "No, that's not why I'm here."

His thick brown eyebrows drew together as uncertainty flashed in his gray eyes. "Then you know Asher Blackstone and now Blackstone Family Enterprise own the hospital."

I nodded gently and pointed at one of the chairs at his desk. "May I?"

"Please do," he said.

I carefully sat in the chair. I kept my lips pressed into a humble smile. He was the chief of surgery, so respect was in order.

"I haven't told anyone, though," I said.

He nodded then smiled. "Good. That was going to be my next question."

We chuckled together. That was a good sign.

"But I'm not here to talk about Jake … I mean Asher," I said.

"Then you know he and I have been friends since childhood?" he asked.

I closed my mouth and swallowed. Apparently, I was done talking about Asher, but he was not.

"Yes."

"And you've received our fellowship offer?"

I had to think. "Oh yes, Deb mentioned it."

He remained pressed back against his chair, studying me shrewdly. It was never good when the chief looked at anyone that way.

"Is everything okay?" I asked, suddenly feeling flushed.

"You do know that Dr. Blackstone will no longer be practicing here come Monday?"

I jerked my head back as if the news had punched me in the nose. "What? Does he know that?" Even though our night had been interrupted by Julia Valentine, I was sure that if Asher knew he was leaving the hospital, that would've been one of the first things he told me.

He shook his head. "No," he said quietly. "So …" He cleared his throat. "My offer to you has nothing to do with him. You're an excellent surgeon."

"Yeah, but honestly if Jake … I mean Asher isn't going to be around, then …"

He held up a hand. "What about Roland Agnew?"

I froze momentarily. "What about Roland Agnew?"

His fingers formed a steeple again, and he tapped the tips together while grinning proudly. "You'll be working directly under Roland and part of EBHI if you accept our fellowship."

"Wow," I mouthed.

Roland Agnew was the world's leading expert in

radiosurgery and neurosurgical oncology. He'd also founded and chaired the Expansive Brain Health Institute, whose headquarters was in Baltimore, Maryland. I had applied for a position with EBHI, along with all the other neurosurgeons in the universe, none of us caring if it was a residency, a fellowship, or an attending position.

I narrowed an eye. "But the EBHI is in Maryland."

"You'll travel to and from." He scratched the side of his face. "It's a once-in-a-lifetime opportunity, isn't it? Not to mention an extremely competitive position. And it's all yours, if you want it."

I cracked a tiny smile. He was being cocky simply because he knew only a fool would turn down the chance to be an EBHI fellow.

"Yes," I said quickly. There was no other answer but that one. "I agree. I'll take it. I'm a fellow—I mean, I'll be a fellow." But then I thought of Asher, and all my excitement dwindled as I collapsed against my chair. "But why does Asher have to leave?"

"Because he's back to being a Blackstone. There's no way he'll be able to practice in a hospital ever again."

"I don't get it," I said, frowning.

His head tilted as he studied me. "You really don't know much about their family, do you?"

I shook my head. "Only what I've learned recently. I'm not good at storing famous people in my knowledge base."

He grunted. "I see. Well, we've already had disturbances because the press and the public are now aware that Asher is on our staff. We've been forced to reassign his surgeries and …" He sighed and shifted in his seat as if talking about Asher was causing him physical pain. "Listen, Asher knows he can't frolic through the hospital as if he's a normal person. And if he thinks he can, then he's deluding himself."

I had a feeling the chief was practicing the argument he'd use to convince Asher to quit his job on me. If he knew the Asher I'd come to know, then he would realize Asher couldn't be forced to do anything he didn't want to do. And my remaining a fellow at the hospital didn't help the chief's case, which was why his claim that the offer had nothing to do with Asher made no sense at all. However, it wasn't my job to figure out who was pulling the strings. The offer had been made. I would've been a fool not to take it. And it was time to focus on my new patient.

"Greg Carroll," I said abruptly.

The chief's brows furrowed. "The American football player?"

"Yes," I said and told him about Greg's symptoms and his need for discretion.

"This hospital has a contract with all local sports teams to report any medical treatment of their players to their organization. It's a standard part of Carroll's contract."

I grunted thoughtfully. "That doesn't sound legal to me."

"It isn't. It's more of a good-faith contract."

I grimaced as I shook my head. "I want to help him. Is there anything you can do to help me do that?"

The chief drew in a deep breath as he pressed his tension-filled lips together. Finally, he released the air trapped in his lungs. "Well, I'm certainly not a stickler for the rules, as you've come to know." He winked at me.

Flutters of hope moved through my belly. "And the hospital is under new ownership. The Blackstones may not agree to the same"—I drew air quotes—"'good-faith deal' as the previous administration."

He stroked his chin, frowning thoughtfully. "True. Very true."

"And he's a VIP."

"Right, right."

I grinned, knowing for certain the chief was going to help. "He'll need a VIP team. People who know how to—"

"I understand, Dr. Ross. Carroll will get his team."

I sat up tall, posturing myself to get moving on it fast. "He's in the hospital, ready to get started."

The door swung open. I twisted around, and the sight of our visitor made my face light up.

"Who's in the hospital, ready to get started?" Asher asked.

"Greg Carroll," Chief Brown said. "And, Ash, we have to talk."

Asher aimed his scowl at me. "Greg Carroll?"

Twelve

PENINA ROSS

Asher stood behind the chair next to me, gripping the top of it. My gaze fell on his hands. He had a tiny scar on the knuckle of his middle finger, and the fuzzy hair that grew there was a lot lighter than the hair on his head. His fingernails were immaculate too. A man with such clean hands—that was sexy. How odd though that I'd never taken a moment to acknowledge such small things about him.

Asher drummed the leather. "Si, we'll talk, but first, I'm going to need to consult with Dr. Ross."

Chief Brown soured his expression. "Consult with Dr. Ross about what exactly?" He eyed Asher as though he was challenging him to come up with a good lie.

"We have to talk about Greg Carroll."

The chief nodded at the empty chair. "Good. Sit. Let's talk."

They smirked at each other until the chief shook his head.

He flung up a hand. "All right, then. Bugger off."

I had just gotten my first view of how close they were as friends. They were two people who could communicate without words—that was pretty close.

"Penina, let's go," Asher said with the sort of gusto reserved for someone who was assured he would get what he wanted.

I took a moment to finish processing what I thought about Asher demanding I go with him. First, the previous night, he'd let me leave and never even called to make sure I'd gotten to bed okay. That was an A-hole move. Secondly, and most importantly, I was in the middle of helping a patient.

"Excuse me, Dr. Blackstone, I presume." I said "presume" because referring to him as Dr. Sparrow still rested on the tip of my tongue.

Asher put his mouth close to my ear. "I'm sorry about last night." He kissed my cheek.

"Um," I said, touching where his lips had left their mark. *What was I going to say?*

"Where's the patient, Dr. Ross?" the chief asked.

I couldn't take my eyes off that hypnotic but cocky grin on Asher's face. He looked different, too —more relaxed and happier.

"First floor, exam room 38," I said finally.

Next, I had to send Greg a text letting him know that, just as he'd snuck into the hospital and kidnapped me out of the hallway, he should be discreet when making his way to the eighth floor, room 809, and Chief Brown would be waiting for him there.

Greg replied quickly. *And you?*

Asher scowled at his reply. "Don't answer that," he said.

I glanced at the chief. I'd never been so casual while in the room with him. It felt odd, and perhaps that was why I was embarrassed to be sitting next to my jealous boyfriend. And the more I thought about how he'd abandoned me the previous night, only to show up the next morning looking as fresh as a powder puff, the more I was sure he had definitely landed himself in the doghouse.

"I can't just ignore a patient," I said, typing out, *Later. I have a consultation.*

"Okay," I said and slipped my phone into my white medical coat then stood up.

My phone dinged again, and without considering how upset answering it would make Asher, I looked to see who it was.

Then I'll wait.

Suddenly pissed, I hit the microphone button and said tersely, "You can't wait. Go meet the chief. Now." I pressed send.

Chief Brown and Asher looked at me as though I had lost my mind.

I'D THOUGHT WE WERE GOING TO ASHER'S OFFICE and had no uncertainty about what we were going to do next. The anticipation made me sensitive down there. He still looked unhappy about my communication with Greg, but that was for him to work out within himself. Greg was my patient. I couldn't just ignore him or pass him off, not yet anyway.

I followed Asher into a stairwell. It was the less populated route to wherever we were going. People would be looking to see us together after the previous night. For a number of reasons, Asher's being a famous Blackstone included, we were the spectacle of the day.

"About last night," I said as we climbed the stairs.

"Penina, I said I was sorry," he said as he stopped in front of a door that always remained locked.

Asher took a ring with six or seven keys on it out of his pocket, found the one he wanted, and unlocked the door. I raised my eyebrows, surprised he already had that level of access.

"If you're apologizing for leaving me wanting you last night, so much so that I gorged on a pint of ice cream—"

He smirked. "You wanted me?"

My eyes grew wider. *Did I confess that out loud?*

Asher pushed the door and held it open. "All you had to do was ask me to stay, and I would've."

I believed him. He would do anything for me, which was an odd thing to feel because I had never been able to rely on anyone other than Christine the way I'd grown to count on him.

I folded my arms. "But what about your ex-girl-friend, my sister?"

"I'll handle her." He pointed his head toward the dusky hallway.

His nearness made me dizzy as I crossed the threshold. "How?" I asked, wondering where he was taking me.

He let the door close and took my hand as we walked quickly down the empty corridor.

"I'll do what it takes."

My curiosity continued to grow as we passed closed unmarked doors. "What does that mean, Jake?"

"It means I'll handle Julia, and there's no need for you to get involved. As a matter of fact …" We reached an elevator, and he pushed the only button associated with it. "I don't want you knowing her."

I put my hands on my hips. "I know Julia and I aren't going to braid each other's hair and swap boyfriend stories, but I'm pretty sure it's not your place to demand that I not get to know her."

"She's dangerous, Penina," he said, raising his voice.

"I gather that by all that you've told me about her." My volume matched his.

"You don't believe me?"

"I believe you."

His features tightened. "Good. Then keep your

distance from her because she will do whatever it takes to come between us."

I sighed sharply. "I understand that, Jake. I mean, Asher. Plus, not only am I a big girl, but I'm pretty astute."

The elevator doors opened, and he extended an arm, holding them open for me.

I stepped in. "And by the way, where are you taking me?"

He entered. "Somewhere private."

As the doors closed, Asher curled an arm around me and tugged me against him. His hot and tasty tongue pushed its way past my lips. I moaned against his mouth as my head spun. His hard body against mine made my legs turn to jelly. Then he put the finishes on our kisses as the door slid open.

Breathing heavily and eyes afire from lust, he said, "I don't want to talk about Julia or Greg right now. Get my drift?"

I gulped and nodded. Then we stepped into the hallway. What happened next occurred lightning fast.

THE BACKS OF MY HANDS ARE PRESSED AGAINST THE wall as Asher pins my arms above my head. Time slows as we stare into each other's eyes. His warm breath collides with mine. It holds the scent of faded mint and an aroma that's naturally his.

"I can't get enough of your face," he whispers.

"Likewise," I say back.

Then our lips connect and stroke each other softly. We add soft, tasty, and hot tongue. My head spins as our kiss deepens. Deeper ... More of his mouth consumes mine. I moan. My cells burst into flames. I throb for him.

I gasp as his solid erection rubs against my pubis, demonstrating what he wants to do next.

"We're not going to make it," he mutters and tugs at the band of my sensible pants. "Take those off."

No need to tell me twice. I slide my trousers down my legs and take my panties with them. When my garments bunch up around my feet, I see that Asher and I are stepping out of our trousers and underwear at the same time.

I can't help myself as I grab his beautiful cock. The tip is glistening with precum. Back and forth, I shift it. It's so solid in my hand.

"Up," he commands, grabbing my ass to hoist me off my feet.

I wrap my legs around his waist. We're like a machine made of instincts. I lean back, and he grabs his erection and stuffs it inside me.

I sigh as he soars through me. He's holding me up by my

thighs, shifting me against him. The sound of sex, my vag colliding with his cock, echoes along with our heavy breathing and moans of pleasure.

I was so eager to have him inside me that I'm already close to climaxing. I tighten around his enormous girth.

"Ah," I cry as he smashes me against him.

"Don't do that. Unless…" he says and jerks my hips against his fullness.

I count them. One, two, three, four, and five thrusts, and he drops his head back and cries out to the Almighty.

OTHER THAN OUR CHESTS RISING AND FALLING AS our breathing slowed, we stood motionless.

"That went fast," he whispered. "I promise to make it up to you tonight."

I tasted his neck, sucking his skin between my teeth, licking as I gently released it. "You gave me nothing to complain about."

"Mmm," he hummed. "So …"

I took large, deep breaths, savoring his scent as I waited for him to finish whatever he was going to say. "So?"

"Were you alone with Greg Carroll?"

I opened my dazed eyes a fraction wider. "Yes."

"I don't like him being around you when I'm not here."

Sniffing, I rolled my eyes.

"Did you just roll your eyes?" Asher leaned back to get a view of my face. I was glad he was smiling, because it meant he couldn't have been serious.

"Probably," I said.

He initiated a tender, heart-soaring kiss. "I love you, Penina," he whispered at the end of it.

Penina, you feel the same way too. Say I love you.

My heart and mind warred with each other. Asher and I had had a tough week. It had been one bombshell after the other. We'd gone from his sort of breaking up with me after the masquerade party, to Gina's showing up and claiming she was his girlfriend, to my believing I might be his sister, to my actual sister's—half-sister's—being his ex-girlfriend. It was a lot, and it made me leery about what could possibly be around the corner, waiting to throw another monkey wrench into our relationship.

"I care for you, too, Jake." I closed my eyes and shook my head. "I mean Asher."

He frowned. "You don't have to say it back."

"No," I said and kissed him tenderly. "I want to say it back. I feel it. But I just learned your real name three days ago."

He tucked a wayward strand of my hair behind my ear and kissed me on the cheek.

I gulped then took a beat to the think of the right reply. "I love Jake Sparrow."

Asher smirked. "And Jake loves you too."

I snorted. "You're so clever."

We kissed again, and when we came up for air, I tossed my head back, and the spottily painted ceiling caught my attention.

"Where are we, anyway?" I asked.

Asher looked up too. "This is where EBHI is going to be."

ASHER LED ME TO AN ON-CALL ROOM EQUIPPED with a shower and three beds. He said it was where he would've taken me if we'd had the willpower to get there. I was moist and sticky between my legs, so I decided to take a quick shower. I was going to take one alone, but as the stream began to flow, I stripped out of my clothes, and so did Asher. We got in the shower together and soaped each other up then shampooed each other's hair. He had a lot of fun stroking my vag all in the name of helping me clean the kitty—and I enjoyed reaping the benefits.

"Tonight, I would like for you to meet my sister. She's in town."

Several of his fingers slid into me, and I lifted my chin and gasped when I answered, "Okay."

Asher's mouth come down over my erect nipple. His tongue swirled around the hardness, sending shivers through me before he gently bit down. I gasped.

"Screw it. Let's just stay here all day."

I chuckled but then released a strong exhale across my lips as his mouth stimulated my nipple again. "You know Chief Brown thinks you're going to quit," I managed to say.

"I know."

Damn, that felt good. "You do?"

His mouth was moving to my other nipple. "I know Si. He's panicking. I'll put his mind to rest. I'm the one who landed this hospital Roland Agnew and Expansive Brain Health Institute. And Roland isn't going to work for anybody but me." He sank as much of my tit as he could into his mouth and kept sucking while guiding me onto a lone shower bench. Asher helped me straddle the bench and laid me back onto the wood. Our dazed eyes remained locked on each other until his hot tongue slid up my slit, then his mouth latched onto my clit.

"Ha!" I cried.

ASHER HAD GOTTEN HARD AGAIN, AND THE ONLY reason we didn't do it again on one of the on-call beds was because our cell phones kept beeping and ringing. Greg was my only patient of the day, and I was grossly neglecting him. I wasn't sure what Asher's day looked like, but I knew for certain it didn't involve any surgeries.

We walked down the empty hallway, going in the opposite direction from where we'd arrived on the floor. Asher and I discussed some probable causes for Greg's memory issues.

"Don't forget to check for syphilis," he said.

I laughed because I could see by his wry smile that he enjoyed saying that.

"I'm serious," he said, faking sounding professional.

"I know."

Asher pressed the down button for the elevator. "That's what you get when you screw around with vagina-addicted athletes—syphilis."

I touched my chest, laughing. "Are you lecturing me?"

The elevator doors opened, and he swept me up in his arms as he brought me inside. "I know you have better taste than that guy."

Beaming at him, I said, "I do."

"Mmm," Jake moaned before he kissed me in his slow, sensual way.

The elevator made it to the ground floor way too fast, and it felt like a mild form of torture to have his lips and tongue abandon mine. But when the door slid open, I was caught off guard by the sight of a dark warehouse.

"What's all this?" I asked after stepping out of the elevator and onto the concrete floor. Large boxes, brand new office furniture, and medical equipment were neatly stacked on tall shelves.

Asher patted an X-ray machine. "All the equipment, furniture, everything's going to be new here. We're making this a cutting-edge hospital."

I ran my hand over the new steel until the tips of my fingers touched his. "Wow."

His hand captured mine, and he interlaced our fingers. My eyebrows flitted upward and stayed there as he drew me against him. "I'm glad you're impressed," he whispered thickly.

Our gazes remained locked until we kissed each other tenderly, keeping it short and sweet so we wouldn't lose track of time again.

He went on to tell me about more of his plans to upgrade the hospital.

"So, is this what you're going to be doing instead of surgeries?" I asked as we walked up a ramp that led to the main hospital.

He shook his head adamantly. "No. But Si is right about one thing—I can't be on staff here. I'll perform high-risk and experimental surgeries through EBHI."

"Ooh," I said, feeling the excitement light up my eyes. "Fun."

We were in a more crowded hallway when he winked at me and said, "You'll be with me."

I bumped into him flirtatiously. "Oh ... You're not hiding your surgeries from me anymore. Remember the last time we were in the OR together?"

He sniffed. "Yes. That was very difficult for me."

I was about to say something witty, but I suddenly noticed how people stared as we passed them.

"However, I want you to work closely with

Roland too. In my opinion, he's the best neurosurgeon in the world. You're going to learn a lot from him, babe," he said as if he didn't notice how everyone was staring at us. He probably didn't care.

"I would love to work closely with him. I mean, just stick me in his armpit twenty-four seven."

He smirked. "As long as there's room for me."

Being self-conscious about all the eyeballs on us didn't stop me from batting my eyelashes at him. "There's always room for you."

We beamed at each other, wearing silly grins.

"Asher Nathaniel Blackstone." The woman had a silky voice and almost sounded as if she had an English accent. Perhaps she was attempting to sound elegant and above us mere mortals.

But I knew exactly who she was when Asher grew stiff. He turned to me, closed his eyes, and shook his head.

"I thought we should talk sooner rather than later, don't you?" she asked even though neither of us had turned to face her.

"I don't want you near her. Go. Now. We'll meet up later," he whispered.

It was as if my feet were on autopilot. My head was climbing a stairway to the moon. His words sat in my brain like a weightless object. That was why I turned to see her. My eyes expanded at the sight of a well-dressed woman in a tight black suit. She wore a red silk shirt under the jacket. Her heels were high, and her skin was dewy and blemish-free, and her makeup perfectly applied. Her long dark hair lay across her shoulders—the strands were silky and soft like she had just left the salon. In a few ways, I saw how we could be related. Our hair color was the same and under all her makeup, I guessed, so were our complexions. I was taller, though. My features were more Ross than whatever she was. However, in the grand scope of it all—her outfit, shoes, fake accent, and the way she stood there, smirking at me—I had glimpsed more differences than similarities.

And she watched me with the same penetrating and assessing glower as I had given her. For a moment, I wondered what she thought.

Asher rubbed my shoulder gently. "Penina, please go."

I looked up at him. He was still facing away from her.

I wasn't one to run from confrontation, but I saw no reason not to respect his wishes. I put my small hand over his large one. "Okay."

His lips came toward mine, and we kissed once,

but that wasn't enough, so we did it two more times quickly. We said we'd see each other later, but I wasn't sure about that. I took another quick glance at Julia. Her arms were crossed, and she smirked at us as if she thought we were putting on a show for her. A sense of dread gripped me because he would be alone with her soon. *Will he kiss her? Remember he loved her?* Those were the questions I asked myself as I walked away.

Thirteen

ASHER BLACKSTONE

She could've at least changed her perfume, but it was still the same syrupy scent that made my stomach turn. She wore the same hairdo too, like a woman who couldn't picture herself without the long tresses of a little girl. Penina was different. She embraced womanhood, and that was sexy as hell. Not only that, but Julia also had the same fabricated walk where she intently put one foot in front of the other. Our pace was brisk, but she didn't miss a beat. Nothing could stop her from strutting like a sex kitten.

"So, Asher, why didn't you return my call?"

I narrowed my eyes, refusing to engage in even the slightest conversation with her. I realized she was taking my temperature and testing my willingness to engage with her.

"Was that my sister? She's … plain."

Again, she was aiming to get a rise out of me. She and I both knew that wasn't the truth.

When I reached my office, I had second thoughts about being alone with her and in close quarters. It would've been beneficial to have witnesses. Si was occupied with Greg Carroll. My brothers weren't around. I glanced at Julia, and her eyebrows flew up.

"Scared?" she asked, smirking.

"Yes," I replied.

"Then you feel the chemistry too."

I grunted bitterly as I stuck my key in the door, trying to take Bryn's advice and be nice to her. I wanted to tell her there could never be chemistry between us. I hadn't known what chemistry felt like until Penina came along. What I felt for Julia was distrust.

I opened the door, and she strolled through, perfecting her sexy strut. When I walked into my office, I didn't close the door all the way. We needed some amount of privacy. I didn't want a passerby overhearing our conversation. I stopped in the middle of the space, making sure there was plenty of room between us. We observed each other. My gaze held suspicion—hers, amusement.

"You're still handsome to the extreme," she said, grinning.

"Why are you here, Julia? And how did you get my number?"

She sniffed. "Do you really have to ask me that? Your whore gave me everything I needed."

I bit down on my back teeth. She knew Gina was no longer practicing prostitution, but she didn't care. Julia needed to view Gina as someone in a lower category of human being than herself. On many occasions, I'd tried to convince Gina that Julia could never be her friend. But Julia was a master manipulator. She knew how to prey on the wounded. With insincerity, she listened to Gina's hardships and offered bad advice, and was disingenuous while consoling her. She even started a sexual relationship with Gina, who used to believe sex, regardless of who she engaged in it with, equated to love. The handful of times Gina and I had sex, though, she never got confused about love, simply because doing it with me made her realize how unworthy of love she felt. Before Penina, my relationships with women amounted to dung. And standing there, looking at a pile of it, I was reminded of that.

"Okay, I'll tell you why I'm here," she said, smirking.

I kept my expression hard. "I'm listening."

She dangled a ring with two keys on it. "I purchased the penthouse from Gina, for one."

I sniffed bitterly. "What do you need the penthouse for?"

"Oh." Her eyes gleamed, proud she made me snap at her. "There you are."

I took a deep breath, rounding my shoulders. *Stay in control, Asher. Don't let her get to you.* "Why do you need it?"

Julia kept sneering. "I have a new job in town."

"Well, it's not for sale."

"The problem is, Gina sold it to me."

I bared my teeth. "The problem is, she can't sell it without my permission."

She smirked, seemingly unaffected by how riled up I was.

"Don't you …" She ran her fingers down her collarbone and unfastened the top button of her blouse. She was on cue. The moment had come for her to use what's between her legs to her advantage. "… miss me? Even a little?"

"No."

"See … I think you do."

"And," I continued, narrowing my eyes to slits, "not only won't I sell my penthouse to you, but Gina no longer owns it. You can set my keys on my desk before you leave my office. And I'll have the locks changed and the security system reset by the time you make it to the end of the hallway."

She stuffed the keys into her blouse. "Come get them."

She was a sad sight, actually. After six years, she was still snatching tricks out of the same tired bag. I'd thought not having Arthur to run to when her blunders needed his fixing would've made her grow up. Apparently not.

"Haven't you noticed how peaceful it is around here? The missing Blackstone brother hasn't left the building, yet there's not a reporter lurking."

I frowned, thoughtful. That was true. I'd walked right through the front entrance that morning, and no one was camping out, trying to capture me with their camera.

"They were here before you arrived. But now they're not."

"Ha! Are you implying that you're responsible for their departure? Because you're definitely responsible for them being here." My accusation hung in the air.

"Humph," she said then watched me with a tight smile. Julia was assessing me, choosing what she would say next carefully.

"Asher, I promise, I never contacted the press."

My face tightened. "I don't believe you."

She shrugged nonchalantly. "To each his own. But don't you want to know where I work?"

"Not really."

"Here at the hospital."

I let out a bitter laugh. If that was the case, then the fix was easy. "You're fired."

She sucked a sharp breath of air between her teeth before she sighed. "Bryn."

Oh … I recognized the tone. The time had come. Julia was on the verge of dropping a bomb. My jaw tightened as I braced myself for impact. "What about Bryn?"

"I know how much you love your sister. And listen, I heard about all the remarkable steps she's taking to change her unremarkable life." She smiled to take credit for her insult.

"What. About. Bryn?"

"Before my father was set up by *your* brother and sent to prison, he left me a goodie basket. And I have all the proof I need against Bryn Blackstone. As you know and I know, she was the one who was dealing drugs at her college and yours. She hired her own chemist to change your highly addictive and synthetic compound. And she made your—oh my god." She closed her eyes, pressing he fingers against her temples. "What was it? I remembered it. It's so fascinating, how smart you people are. It was Xynalycophene Yellow."

I felt all the tension drop out of my face. *How did Arthur know that?* We all knew he had something on Randolph. *Was that it?*

"That was why your father had Bryn pulled out of college after her freshman year. Or was it Jasper who did the pulling? He's always been your real daddy, hasn't he? I wouldn't be surprised if he screwed Amelia. I mean, they were just so weirdly close."

Speechless, I shook my head.

"But nobody has to know what Bryn did if Jasper wants to deal."

Finally, we were getting to the point of her showing up in New Orleans and scheming herself into a job in my hospital. I folded my arms. "What do you want?"

"My father's innocent of all charges." Uncertainty flashed in her eyes when she said that.

A bitter laugh escaped me. "Have you consulted with your brother?"

"He's a peon. Your father was the pervert, not mine. Your brother ruined his life, and mine."

I couldn't stop shaking my head. I hadn't thought about Julia since I became Jake Sparrow. But I wasn't surprised she was still singing the hymn of her father's innocence. But I wasn't invested in what Julia believed. I could give a damn. There was one thing for certain, he was a rapist and murderer, and it wasn't just Jasper who would make sure Arthur Valentine would die in prison for his crimes, but Spencer and me as well. There was something else going on inside me. The longer I observed her sameness and smelled her syrupy perfume, the less angry I became.

"Get out of my office, Julia." I would've called HR and security right then and there and had her fired and thrown off the premises, but I had to consult Jasper first. So far, we had gone virtually untouched by my father's sins. Thanks to my brothers' efforts, the public had never held us accountable. But the cover-up and Bryn's mistake could make us all look rotten to the core. She had been

young and rebellious back then. I had to do whatever it took to make sure her actions didn't come
back to bite her and me in the ass.

Julia's smirk revealed that she knew she had me
in checkmate, at least for now.

"I want my penthouse, and I'll keep my job,"
she said as if she had no doubt I would give her
what she wanted. Then she took a few steps forward
to stand right in front of me. Her breath smelled
the same, turning my stomach.

Then, to my utter surprise, she squeezed my
cock. "And I want your golden cock." She sighed as
though touching me was getting her off.

I gripped her wrist, wishing I could crush the
bone. "Don't you ever touch me. That's reserved for
your sister."

There it was, the flash of anger—no, it was rage
—in her eyes. "Let go of me," she said with
clenched teeth and tried to snatch her wrist out of
my grasp.

I wasn't ready to let go yet. "You should walk
away while you still have what you still own." Then
I let go of her.

Julia tugged the hem of her suit jacket and
pulled her shoulders back. Then her lips slowly

formed a smirk. "See you around, Dr. Sparrow—
and my sister too." She winked.

I stared daggers at her as she strolled out of my
office, but I kept my composure, not wanting her to
see that I was indeed alarmed. *How did Valentine
know about Bryn?* There was supposed to be no paper
trail left behind. *How did Arthur Valentine find one?* I
almost didn't believe her, but still, it would've been
negligent to ignore her threat. So I took my phone
out of my pocket and called my brother, Jasper.

———

PENINA WAS THE SECOND PERSON I LOOKED FOR. No
one I asked had seen her. I found Deb at the care
station, combing over charts, and asked her too.

"No, but don't you feel you owe me a conversation?" she asked.

"Not now, Dr. Glasgow." I was shorter with her
than I wanted to be.

"Don't you want to know why I don't know
where she is?"

I tensed up. She had regained my full attention.
"I'm listening."

"She's no longer a resident as of"—she checked

her watch—"twenty minutes ago. She's now a fellow. As always, it's who you know, or more."

Whoa. She sneered like she wanted to spit in my face. I'd never seen Deb that angry. The time she came to my office when I was with Penina, I'd known what her visit was concerning. However, Penina would never have guessed that her boss was coming to make her play for me. Deb was always acutely aware that I was within proximity. Even seconds ago, when I walked into the care station to find Penina, she'd gone rigid and doubled her efforts to pretend as though she hadn't noticed me.

Her reaction toward me was fine. Over time, my newness would wear off, and she would point her attraction elsewhere. However, facing Julia that morning had incited an aggression within me that had been long dormant. I found myself wanting to remind Deb of who was in charge and that there was no one higher to report to than me. But I took a beat to get a grip on myself. Even though my pervading desire to torture Julia, the feeling that kept me tethered to her, had dissipated, she still brought out the worst in me.

"Do you think it's fair what you said about Dr. Ross?" I asked, keeping cool, calm, and collected.

"She's suddenly Dr. Ross again and not Penina?"

She was snarling, showing teeth, and that discombobulated me. I cleared my throat, wondering if we would be able to reach an amicable conclusion to this conversation.

"To me, she's both, and she's been saving your department's ass for the better part of three years, performing surgeries that only full-fledged residents should've. She finally gets a break, and you want to attribute it to her relationship with me?" I leaned closer to Deb so she wouldn't miss one word of what I was going to say. "And we are in a relationship. I love her, and that's that." I stood up straight.

Deb's face turned as her gaze bounced around the hallway. I waited patiently, giving her more time to think before responding. Then she coughed into her fist to clear her throat.

"Well, I still don't know where Dr. Ross is. I haven't seen her since this morning. But—" she said in a way that seemed like maybe it hurt to let go of her self-righteous condemnation of Penina—"I agree. Dr. Ross has been a credit to our department and to the hospital in general. She deserves that fellowship."

She glared at me as if she wanted me to get away from her. I was happy to oblige.

After a sharp nod I said, "Thanks, Dr. Glasgow," and shuffled up the hallway.

Satisfied it ended amicably between Glasgow and me, I went to Si's office, but Penina wasn't there either. I went to the eighth floor, room 809, where he was supposed to have met up with Greg Carroll. The room was empty. I stopped to think. I was in a race to keep Penina from running into Julia. Only God knew what Julia would say to her. Julia could vex anyone, even if he or she had the resolve of the Dalai Lama.

Standing in the middle of another hallway, unsure of my next move, I took my phone out of my coat pocket and sent a text to Si, asking where the hell he was.

I'm in the planning meeting, brother. Where are you? he replied.

Agitated, I rubbed the back of my neck. *That's right. I was supposed to be there.*

WHERE'S PENINA? I TYPED.

With Carroll. They've gone to East River Medical Care Center for privacy. Get over here.

. . .

"Damn!" I shouted loudly enough to shatter glass.

A few heads poked out of rooms.

I turned away from them and stomped toward the closest elevator as I called Penina and once again reached her voice mail.

"Call me when you get this," I said.

On the way up to the top floor, I decided to look on the bright side. She wouldn't be running into Julia while at the private facility. And I trusted she wouldn't take the bait for whatever trap Carroll was laying. The guy was more transparent than plastic wrap.

Before I entered my first meeting of the day, Jasper texted me, asking Bryn and me to meet him at the family mansion in the Garden District for lunch and a meeting at noon. He said he wanted to lay it all out on the table—no more secrets, no more ghosts.

I'll see you at noon, I texted back.

As a man in love with the woman I wanted to spend the rest of my life with, I agreed with Jasper. All that could destroy our family had to be immediately dealt with.

Fourteen

PENINA ROSS

It was odd how quickly the chief had tried to shuffle us out of the hospital. Earlier, when I arrived on the eighth floor, he was in the hallway with Samantha Gladstone, head of communications and community outreach. They stopped their conversation to look at me. Before I could join them, she said thank you to him without giving me a second look then spun on her heel and walked away. I wasn't offended by her lack of manners. Samantha was snooty and barely spoke to anyone. I always wondered how someone so cold and unlikable could be in charge of the hospital's image and outreach.

Regardless, the chief handed me my contract

for the fellowship and asked me to sign while we were standing there.

"I never sign anything without reading it thoroughly," I said.

"What? You don't trust us?" he asked, giving me his charming smile.

I looked off in the direction Samantha had walked. "What were you and Sam Gladstone talking about?"

He pressed his lips together, eyeing me keenly. The way he looked at me made me nervous. I felt out of line, questioning him about what was more than likely a private matter that didn't involve me. I didn't want him to think that since I was in the bed and heart of the head honcho, I'd become too big for my britches.

I shook my head. "Forget about it."

"Samantha has hired Julia Valentine as her new PR director."

Nearly choking with shock, I took a step back. "Julia Valentine?" I heard myself say her name, but I was so detached from my body that I wasn't quite sure the voice was mine.

"Yes. But don't worry. You won't run into her today, and count Greg Carroll as your last patient before you take sabbatical."

"Sabbatical?" I asked, still dazed by the previous revelation about Julia.

The chief put a hand on by back, guiding me toward room 809. "I wasn't able to procure the sort of discretion Mr. Carroll requested at this facility, anyway—especially with what's going on with Asher and the Blackstones. But I was able to call in a favor at East Lake. You know where that is, don't you?"

I nodded.

"A team will be waiting for you when you arrive. I called down to the motor pool. Take one of the hospital vehicles. Any questions?"

I was still stuck on Julia being employed by the hospital. "Does Asher know Julia works here?"

"I'm not sure, but he will soon. But hear me well—" He put a hand on my other shoulder, garnering steady eye contact. "Don't worry about Julia Valentine." He checked over both shoulders. "The Blackstones will foil whatever she's planned."

I gasped, eyes bulging. "She's planning something?" My voice was so small.

"Julia Valentine always has a plan. But as I said, you have nothing to worry about." He nodded, smiling. "Today could be your last day, Dr. Ross. That's good news, is it not?"

"I guess so." I swallowed the lump in my throat. "All I have to do is figure out what's wrong with Greg Carroll and then I'm free?"

Chief Brown handed me the order for Greg's services, which included my point of contact. "Then you're free. Good luck," he said and walked off.

I watched him until he turned the corner. Suddenly, the fact that I was one patient away from sabbatical struck me. Soon, I would be able to sleep in and make love to Asher without having to worry about my shift the next morning. No more night calls either. The only reason I'd come in at night was if I was needed for surgery. Soon, I would be free, which was why I was smiling from ear to ear when I opened the door.

Greg, who was standing in front of the window, twisted around to face me.

"There you are," he said then frowned. "Your hair's wet. Did you take a shower?"

My mouth fell open, then I closed it as I touched my head. *The chief must've noticed too.* No wonder everyone was staring at Asher and me. We looked like we'd just showered, and it didn't take a rocket scientist to guess we had taken one together.

GREG WOULD NOT QUIT ASKING ME WHY I'D TAKEN a shower. All I had to do was tell a lie to make him stop, but I was up to my eyeballs in lying by keeping secrets, both Asher's and mine, so I just shrugged and said, "Because I wanted to."

We were at the entrance of the carpool when Greg frowned at the line of white sedans, vans, and trucks.

"What are we doing here?" he asked.

"I'm checking out a car so I can drive us to the medical facility."

"I'm a big guy, and those are small cars," he groused. "We'll take my SUV."

"I thought you wanted to be discreet."

"I do, but come on." He waved me away from the chain-link fence that surrounded the carpool. "My car. Let's go."

My feet remained posted to the concrete. "I can't. You're a patient and one who woke up this morning and couldn't remember his name. You've already endangered everyone—"

"Okay. I heard you. Then you drive. I ride."

He tossed me the keys. Thank goodness I had good reflexes, because I caught them.

Still, I pressed my lips together, feeling anxious. Driving Greg's car felt as if I was crossing a line from professional to way too personal.

"I'm not sitting in anything behind that fence. So make up your mind. Are you coming with me or not?"

I DIDN'T NEED TO PROGRAM THE NAVIGATIONAL system, since I'd been to the private facility a dozen times over the course of my residency. The place was high tech and the people that worked there highly skilled. They worked fast too. Whatever was wrong with Greg, I would have a good indication of what that was before we left the facility.

However, I'd never understood why anyone needed or wanted a car as enormous as Greg's SUV. It was a Hummer, and driving it made me feel as if we were part of a military coalition with orders to seize the city. But goodness, driving it sure was fun. It was as if I were sitting on top of the world, and the wheels rolled down the street smoothly, just like we were riding on butter.

"So, who did you take a shower with? Dr. Blackstone?" Greg asked.

I jerked my head around to glance at him then quickly put my eyes back on the road. "What?" *How the hell does he know Dr. Sparrow is Dr. Blackstone?*

"Surprised I know who your boyfriend really is?"

"Very surprised."

"It's all over the news. He's big time. The Blackstones are like the Kennedys. I'm surprised we don't have a motorcade following us right now. I think it's because you're with me. I'll keep you safe."

"Why would I need a motorcade?"

"Aren't you married to Asher Blackstone?"

I sniffed. "No."

"Oh," he said as if he was titillated by my answer.

"Then you're his girlfriend and not his wife. You know what that means, don't you?"

"The fact that I'm not married to him?"

"You're fair game."

That we were having that conversation felt surreal. "What brought all this on, anyway?" I asked.

"Brought all what on?"

"Last night at the party, you showed no interest in me. Now you're claiming I'm fair game?"

When I glanced at Greg, he was smirking.

"That was tactic. It didn't work. You left with the wrong guy."

I did a double take. "You mean I left with my boyfriend."

"A boyfriend is not——"

"A husband. Yes. You said that already. And that might be part of your belief system, but it's not part of mine."

"Did you shower with him? I know you were with him earlier. He wears this cologne. I can smell him on you."

I sniffed one of my shoulders then the other. "Cologne?"

"Oh, that's a good sign," he said, cheesing.

"What's a good sign?"

"You don't know how his cologne smells."

"Maybe it's not cologne you're smelling."

"It's cologne."

"No, it's not."

"Ask him. Call him now. Let him know you're with me."

I shook my head like a rattle. "Enough about Jake … I mean Asher."

Greg sneered at me as if my blunder was the reason why he believed Asher and I would never go the distance. However, he was wrong. I would never judge Asher for seeing how it felt to live as someone else. It was a bold move, and frankly, I wished I'd thought of it. *What would it have been like to be Raine Waters or Rose Redd instead of Penina Ross? Would either of those women have become a surgeon?* Both sounded like stripper names, and I wasn't stripper material.

"What about you, Greg?" I asked, thankful that we were almost at our destination.

"What about me?" he asked.

"What happened between you and your last girlfriend?"

"Ha," he said, quickly turning to look out the window. "Girlfriend? I don't do girlfriends. I'm the dope who goes straight from meeting them to asking them to marry me then calling off the engagement. But you, you're a different caliber of woman." He faced me, and even though I wouldn't look at him, I could feel his eyes undressing me. "I'd follow through with you. We'd get married and move to Vermont. We'd own an apple farm, raise five kids, all of which I would definitely have a lot of fun impregnating you with." He sucked air between his teeth, and through my peripheral vision I saw him grab his package.

I couldn't believe him. My mouth couldn't close, and words wouldn't form. I couldn't even unpack all he had said. But there was something I had to say. Miss Nice Doctor had to be locked in a cage, and stern and professional Dr. Ross had to be released.

"Greg, you're making me uncomfortable with your level of flirting. I mean, impregnating me? I'm your doctor and may be your surgeon. Do you want me to help you with your brain? Or do I assign you to another doctor and keep my distance from you?"

I forced my eyes to remain on the road as he sat quietly. Anticipation hung in the air. *Is he going to respect my wishes or not?* I glanced at him after I turned in to the parking lot.

He was nodding thoughtfully.

"What's it going to be?" My tone remained stern.

"I understand. I'm coming on strong as hell because I know there's no beating a Blackstone. But I wish I had taken you from Rich when I had the chance. He didn't deserve you. We'd be married by now." He said that as though he actually believed it.

"No, we wouldn't be married."

"What?"

"We wouldn't be married." I pulled into a parking space next to the entrance.

"Why do you say that?" He sounded disappointed.

I put the oversized SUV in park, turned off the engine, and made sure we kept steady eye contact. "Because I'm a surgeon, Greg. I'm not a woman who gives birth to five kids and lives on an apple farm. You're infatuated by my looks, and that's okay. If that's the kind of person you are, then so be it. But once you learned who I really am, how inaccessible someone like me can be, and how I will always choose my career over all you say you want out of life, you'd run away from me like your feet were on fire." And that I was one hundred percent sure of.

Greg stared at me, blinking hard. It was as though he was rattled by what I had just said. I sat up taller, as if to show I was standing behind every word. It was best not to sugarcoat the truth.

"I guess you're right," he said finally.

"I *am* right. Who I am is why Rich and I broke up."

"Part of it," he said. "Rich doesn't know how to be faithful to a beautiful, smart, and classy woman like you. He's already cheating on Court," he said as he opened the door. "Stay seated."

He jumped out of the passenger seat, trotted

around the front of his SUV, and opened my door. Then he held out his hand.

I hesitated but took it. "Thanks."

He smiled as he helped me out of the vehicle. "You're welcome. Now let's go see what's wrong with my brain, Dr. Ross."

Fifteen

PENINA ROSS

The professional staff got right to work. As Greg was prepped for an fMRI, X-rays, and a CT scan, I ran through his symptoms for my team of specialists. They asked me questions and made suggestions as we considered some causes and ruled out other possibilities. I had never considered infectious disease until Asher mentioned it earlier, so I ordered a full panel of blood tests to check for everything under the sun that could be associated with memory loss.

Three hours later, Greg and I were alone in the examination room. I'd just told him that he indeed had mild CTE, which was not enough to cause his symptoms. His CTE couldn't be helped though, since he'd been playing football since high school.

Over the course of time, his condition would climb to the higher stages. It was up to him to make a choice about whether his brain was ultimately worth sixty million dollars.

"If that's not it, then what is it?" he asked.

I pressed my lips together and shook my head out of frustration. "There has to be something you're not telling me. It's not syphilis …"

He lurched back. "Syphilis?"

"I had to check. You don't have a blood clot or a tumor. We checked for steroids that we know cause brain impairment. Your vitamin B-12 levels are high, which, from your intake questionnaire, was to be expected. You don't have hypothyroidism. The only thing I can think of is that you're truly faking it just to get close to me."

He looked baffled while shaking his head adamantly. "Granted, Dr. Ross, I like being close to you, but that's not it. Something's wrong."

I studied him as he massaged his temples. *Am I missing something?* Maybe his CTE was more progressive than the scan indicated.

Sighing, I sat down in the chair across from him and crossed my legs, setting his chart on my lap. I pinched my lips together as I contemplated what to do next. I certainly didn't want to leave the high-class facility without a final diagnosis. If it couldn't be made at the East Lake facility, then EBHI would be our next option, only we couldn't keep his treatment a secret from his team, the Voyagers.

"And the team doctors ran the scans on your brain?" I asked.

"Yeah, and I know they saw the CTE. I'm over it. I'm quitting."

"You're giving up the money, huh?"

"They've already paid me five million. That's all I need."

I nodded then narrowed an eye. "No steroids, huh?"

"No," he said, frowning and looking off.

"You don't sound sure about it."

"I've been given vitamins. Josh said there were no steroids in them. And you said my vitamin levels looked good."

I perked up, shuffling through my paperwork to find Greg's intake form. "Except your B12 levels. But you said you had a B-12 drip two days ago. I would watch those if I were you. What other kinds of vitamins are you taking?"

"Multivitamins. But they're not the reason from my episodes. They're vitamins, for goodness sake."

I frowned, reading through the blocks again.

He'd never mentioned any vitamins other than the drip. That was a big miss by Dr. Beals, the internal medicine doctor. But as part of the diagnostic team, I should've followed up on the question. Normally, I would have.

"And Dr. Beals never asked you about any daily supplements that you might be taking?"

His lips settled into a coy grin. "The cute blonde."

I wrinkled an eyebrow. "Were you flirting with her?"

"No."

I didn't believe him. From personal experience, I knew how strong he could come on to a woman he was attracted to. He probably made her feel flustered, which was why she got through the test as fast as she could. But there was no need to point fingers. Finally, we had a lead on a possible cause.

"When was your last dosage?" I asked.

"This morning. You're barking up the wrong tree, Doc. Those vitamins make me feel great."

I tilted my head. "They do?"

He grimaced, appearing annoyed by my questioning the viability of his supplements.

"How can I get my hands on these vitamins?"

"I have some. I take them three times a day."

"Would you mind giving me your next dosage?"

He stiffened. His brow wrinkled then evened out.

"It's not a popper, right? It's just a vitamin. Unless you're addicted to these vitamins." My tone sounded suggestive.

Finally, Greg dug into his pocket and took out a small pill box. After he gave me his next dose, I explained how most people heard the word "vitamin" and thought what they were taking was good for them. However, not all vitamins were healthful, and most were made of synthetic substances.

"Dr. Ross," he said as my hand gripped the doorknob.

I turned around to look at him.

"Thank you. I owe you dinner. How about tonight?"

Chastising him for flirting, I wiggled my finger at him as I walked out of the room. "Stay put."

DR. BEALS CONFIRMED THAT GREG HAD BEEN flirtatious. She also confessed that his hunkiness may have been distracting. Regardless, she rallied her troops and got to work on his case.

Since we were certain no surgery was warranted, my services wouldn't be needed. However, curiosity made me stick close to the team. The lab had everything they needed to separate the substances and learn which active ingredients were contained in the vitamin.

An hour later, we were back in the SUV, and Greg drove because we were certain he wouldn't have another episode of memory loss. During the team's post-diagnostic follow-up, I learned each memory lapse occurred up to half an hour after he took a vitamin. The time of reaction depended on how fast his body metabolized the supplement. At one point, he'd added an extra dosage to his routine, simply because it gave him an extra boost of energy.

"Did they say the supplement contained six statins?" he asked.

He was driving too fast, and it was getting to me.

"Could you please slow down?" I asked while listening to the third and final message from Asher.

In each, he asked that I return his call as soon as possible. He sounded worried, and I didn't think it was because I was with Greg. That sucky feeling that came over me when he'd walked off with Julia was back in spades. But he had left me three messages since then, which meant he hadn't fallen into her clutches. So I relaxed a bit, deciding to put my conversation with Greg regarding informing his team about the harmful supplements on ice while I called Asher to let him know I was okay. But before I could make the call, my phone rang. I gasped when I saw who it was. After forcing myself to breathe, I answered.

"Hi, Christine."

"Your mother's been found." The fact that she got straight to her point worried me.

I looked at Greg with wide eyes as I pressed my hand on my chest.

"Is she alive?" I whispered past my tight throat.

"Everything okay?" Greg asked, splitting his attention between my face and the road.

I didn't know how to respond, so I just kept staring at him.

"She's alive," Christine said, her tone sharp enough to slice through an iceberg. Then she gave a long sigh. "Get ready for this, darling—and I'm sorry I have to tell you this, but for the sake of full disclosure, you have to know."

I leaned forward, hugging the phone closer to my ear. "Know what?"

Then Aunt Christine told me everything, including where I would be able to find my mom. She said she had chosen to wash her hands of Mary, and it took every ounce of willpower to give me the option to make the same decision for myself.

"I hope you do the same, but you have to choose for yourself."

She was right. I thanked her and told her I loved her. Christine said we were going to call each other every week, spend every holiday together, and finally act as if we were family.

I loved hearing that, but I also knew Christine's proclamation was a big "Screw you" to my mom for abandoning us not only once but twice.

"Um…" I said, grimacing at my phone, trying to remember the last remark Greg had made. "Yes, statins, beta blockers, and substances—we had to make some calls to figure out what they were and who manufactured them. Are all your team members taking them?" I was proud of myself for being able to get all of that out, even though I wanted to break down and cry.

"Beautiful?" His voice was calm and steady.

I stopped my shaky fingers from searching the internet for a flight to Madison, Wisconsin, and blinked at Greg. "Huh?" It was as if he were sitting a million miles away from me.

"Who just called you, and why are you searching for an airplane ticket?"

"My aunt. My mother is living in Madison, Wisconsin. I haven't seen her since I graduated from high school."

We whipped around another corner. If I were in my right mind, I would have asked him to take the next corner a little slower.

I found Asher's name on my recent call screen and tapped it. The line rang four times before going to voice mail.

"Asher, I just learned about my mother. I'm going to the airport. I'm flying out to Wisconsin. I'll see you when I get back. Love you."

Greg checked all the mirrors carefully as he pulled over.

When the oversized vehicle was safely sitting along the side of the road, he turned his entire body to face me. "Do you want me to take you to the airport?"

I hated that I was so frantic. I shook my head as I tried to calm down. "No, take me to my place. I have to pack a small bag first."

"Dr. Ross … Penina. Can I call you Penina?"

I nodded rapidly.

"You have to calm down. I got this. I promise you—I got this."

I grimaced, wondering what he meant by that. Then Greg made a call on his console to a "charter service."

"I'm booking a flight to"—he looked at me—"where again?"

My mouth was caught open. *Should I, or shouldn't I?* Then the words started to form. "Madison, Wisconsin," I said reluctantly. It was a bad idea to get on Greg's airplane, knowing how much he liked me, but the sooner I reached my mother, the better.

"Return date?" the woman asked.

"Tonight," I said.

I didn't need to stay long. I had to see Mary and let her know that I knew she had done exactly what Asher did. She'd changed her name, but she had also gone several steps farther. Mary had become Elizabeth Thomas from Little Rock, Arkansas. She had two small children and a husband who was an airplane mechanic. I wanted to lay eyes on Elizabeth Thomas and tell her that I was aware of what she had done, and that from that moment onward, we were dead to each other.

A LITTLE OVER AN HOUR LATER, WE WERE IN A private airplane on the tarmac, waiting for the aircraft to finish being prepared, when Asher returned my call. My hands were still shaky, and I had to constantly beat back the urge to cry as I told him how my aunt's private investigator had miraculously found my mother, who had a brand-new identity and a new set of kids.

Then the pilot announced we were finally ready for takeoff.

"Are you on an airplane already?" Asher asked.

Filled with dread, I closed my eyes and sighed, knowing he wasn't going to like what I said next. "Greg chartered a flight for us."

"Us?" His voice boomed so loudly that I had to move the phone away from my ear. "You're alone with that guy?"

The aircraft was moving, and the flight attendant had set the coffee that I ordered in front of me.

"It's okay." I narrowed an eye at my fellow passenger. "Greg and I have an understanding."

"You think that's helping, Penina?"

I heaved a sigh. "I love you and only you, Jake."

I cursed under my breath. I was volatile, very unstable, and I knew it. "I meant Asher."

"Madison, Wisconsin?" he asked.

"Yes."

"Give me the address."

I turned away from Greg, who was smirking. "What?"

"Never mind. My investigator was the one who helped your aunt's detective."

I tried to scoot to the edge of my seat, but the seat belt restrained me. "What? Why didn't you tell me that?"

"Because it was me helping you out. It was no big deal."

I closed my eyes as I shook my head. "You could've said something."

"We're next in line for takeoff," the pilot said as if he were announcing a sunny day in Whoville. "Please turn off your laptops, make sure your device is in airplane mode, and enjoy the ride, Greg Carroll, greatest offensive tackle in the league."

Greg crossed his arms and barked out a loud laugh. The compliment clearly made him feel special. I could tell by the look on his face that moments like that, for him, were worth the CTE.

"You have to turn it off," Greg mouthed then winked.

He was relishing the moment. I bet he felt like a winner, and Asher was the loser. I should've thought it through, but it was too late now.

"Asher, I have to go."

"I'll see you soon," he said and ended our call.

I smiled at Greg. "Love you too."

"He's not mad?" Greg asked as I pulled the phone away from my ear.

"Nope," I said a little too optimistically.

He grunted thoughtfully. I didn't think he believed me, but I wasn't going to give him any indication that Asher was pissed.

"You love him, huh?"

My smile intensified. "Very much."

His eyes narrowed, then after a moment of studying me, he grunted again.

I rolled my eyes. *Whatever.*

Sixteen

ASHER BLACKSTONE

TWO HOURS AGO

I sat at the table with Jasper and Bryn. We were in the den at the back of the house, sitting beneath a coffered ceiling. Nourished trees surrounded the large circular windows. The only reason I noticed those details was because Bryn mentioned how pleasant the room felt for once.

We'd just finished eating grilled salmon with roasted carrots, tomatoes, and baked rosemary new potatoes for lunch. Bart, the family chef, who had been with us since I was a kid, had prepared our meal. I'd forgotten how tasty his food was.

While eating, we mainly talked about Bryn's plan

to work with Spencer and his wife, Jada, in their efforts to fundraise for the Spencer and Jada Blackstone Indemnity Fund. Spencer planned to use family investment funds to pay those who had been abused by our father or were close relatives of the abused. However, they had expanded the mission of their non-profit organization to include those who were not associated with Randolph but had also become victims of the sex trade, and their families. And it was for that reason they had chosen to procure outside financial resources and volunteer services as a means of support.

Jasper listened as I updated him on my morning meetings and how fast we were moving to advance the facility, recruit new physicians and nurses, and improve patient services. We discussed administrative hires, including Si staying on as chief of surgery. I presented some options to Jasper, and he listened attentively, asking the right questions regarding their backgrounds and experiences.

The servers had finished collecting our plates, and we were drinking coffee for dessert when Jasper asked the one question I'd known would eventually find its way to my ears.

"I'm not particularly interested in hospital administration," I replied in response to taking the position as CEO of the hospital. I was a surgeon, not a paper pusher. "Although I want to know everything that's going on."

"That's fair," Jasper said.

Then we tossed names across the table. I wasn't shocked that he knew who the major players were in the medical institution industry. When Jasper entered an industry, he made a point to know everything about it.

I knew the pleasantries were over after we fell silent and Jasper's stern gaze shifted between Bryn and me. The time had come to discuss why we were meeting at the mansion and not at one of the best restaurants in the city.

"About Julia's threat," he said, then laced his fingers together in front of him. As I recalled, that was a good sign. It meant he wasn't speaking from a position of vulnerability.

Bryn drew up her mouth as if she were smelling something bad. "She's awful."

I waited for her to add more, like calling Julia a cunt or a bitch and saying she should burn in hell. But that was it. "She's awful" was as far as the new Bryn was willing to take an insult, and it was a true statement.

"We don't need to rehash what occurred back then—the Redmond College ordeal," Jasper said.

Bryn and I looked at each other. We were at the start of discussing one of the biggest mistakes of our lives. I had been a chemistry student. Even though Bryn and I were born on the same day, I was starting my junior year at university when she was a freshman. I was young and also pissed off at everything that had breath and a brain. My anger made me make bad, wrong decisions. It was the only way to quell my heat. I manufactured a recreational drug.

Before she went off to college for the first time, Bryn and I gave my invention a try. If we died, then so what—we would finally be free of the Blackstone mansion and our father's control. I was halfway hoping Xynalycophene Yellow, which we called HOE, short for Heaven on Earth, would kill me, but it didn't. Bryn and I enjoyed the high of our lives. When she went off to Redmond College, she asked if I could make more HOEs, and she would sell them.

We were in the backyard, smoking by the oak tree across from the guest lodge. The lodge was where we got high, brought our sex buddies, and sometimes partied.

. . .

Inhaling on the cig, I look at her with one eye narrowed, barely believing she asked me to do that. "You want me to be a drug dealer?"

She slaps herself on the chest. "I'm the dealer. You're my manufacturer and supplier. I'll give you a cut."

"I don't want a cut."

Then she pushes me in the shoulder, and I fall off balance but quickly recover.

"Come on, Ash," she explodes then displays one of my pills between her fingers. "Either you stock me with this, or I'll find someone to tell me what's in it, and I'll make my own."

THAT WAS HOW IT HAPPENED. I REMEMBERED MY deliberation process because I'd relived that moment over a thousand times. First, I wasn't used to saying no to Bryn. So I used the excuse of not wanting anyone to learn what was in my formula to give her what she wanted.

Whenever I thought back to that day, I saw myself telling her to go screw off. But I didn't do that, and she'd dealt what I made. Then she met a guy who talked her into changing with my recipe. I didn't know what she'd done until the second user overdosed.

It was the biggest mistake we ever made. I could've gone to jail for a long time, and so could she. But Jasper, who had only been in his early twenties, made it all go away. And I never asked how he'd done it, simply because I took him for granted. Fixing our father's pathological actions and ours was my older brother's responsibility.

When I looked back on Jasper's role in our family, I saw the abuse and the burden. Being a neurosurgeon had taught me a lot about the brain —without it, we were not ourselves. Our father molded his older son into his greatest asset, but not out of love. Jasper was supposed to be his tool and ultimately his weapon. It never happened the way Randolph planned, though—not exactly. Jasper had never been our father's ally. He was always the fox in the henhouse. I never knew why Jasper so often operated against our father until I read *The Dark Blackstones*, which was a book about our family, written by Jasper's wife.

Jasper's laser focus was set on me. "When you told me about Julia's threat, I did some rechecking. I always wondered about Brian Moore." He looked at Bryn when he said that name.

Her jaw dropped, and she swallowed.

"Remember him?" he asked her.

Bryn's pale skin had turned deathly white as she nodded stiffly.

"I figured the only way Valentine could've known about the drugs was if he sent Moore to you. So I checked."

She gasped. "Brian was paid by Valentine?"

"Yes."

"Do you just have a hunch, or have you already confirmed it?" I asked.

"It's confirmed."

Impressed, I raised my eyebrows, nodding. "That was fast."

Jasper shrugged. "It was easy. And what I've done about it was easier."

"What did you do?" Bryn asked.

Jasper clamped his lips together and narrowed his eyes. She must've known she wouldn't receive an answer. I'd changed, she'd changed, and so had Spencer, but Jasper hadn't.

"So, I can fire Julia?" I asked. I couldn't wait to send her packing.

"Monday morning. She's going to receive a package from you, Asher."

I frowned. "A package from me?"

He sat back in his seat, pushing his steepled fingers against his chin. "Yes, the morality clause in the Valentine trust prohibits funds being used for bribery or extortion, which means Julia is on the verge of losing whatever little she receives from that financial source. And now that we have Penina, it's a done deal."

"Oh no," I said, shifting abruptly, picturing how that was going to play out. "Leave her out of it."

"Do you really think Julia's going to let Dr. Ross skip off into the sunset?" Jasper asked. "The answer is no. Which is why we have to strike before she does."

I closed my mouth, and swallow as my gaze ping-ponged between Jasper and Bryn.

"Julia is the queen of vengeance and self-dealing," Bryn said, I suspected in an effort to make me wake up and smell the snake.

I opened my eyes after absorbing her words, and then nodded.

"Excellent. The plan is set. Now sell it," Jasper said. "I also figured out Julia was the one who told Boomer that you and Bryn had murdered Randolph."

He had moved so rapidly to the next subject that my head was still spinning.

"That makes sense," Bryn said, shaking a finger. "Because Valentine never knew Father was in a semi-coma for months before he died."

"True," Jasper said. "You want to know who Julia extorted?"

"Who?" Bryn asked, frowning curiously.

"The nurse, Laura, and Dr. Carlisle."

Bryn and I looked at each other. Suddenly, the dread of telling Penina that my brother, who she never met, was planning on giving her all of Julia's money had left me. I swallowed the lump lodged in my throat as I saw the incident replay in my head.

His bedroom at the mansion. The respirator. Father opening his eyes. The beeping going off as he takes his last breaths. To stop the noise, Bryn rushes over and pulls the plugs.

"Are you goddamn crazy?" I ask.

Her eyes expand, warning me to keep quiet.

Father is sucking air. We're aware that Laura, the nurse, should be called into the room. It's her job to resuscitate him. I refuse to watch my father struggle like a fish out of water. Instead, I keep my curious gaze on Bryn. She wants him dead. I've asked her more times than I can remember if Father ever crossed the line with her. She's always denied it.

Watching her, I don't believe her. She was lying. Father indeed crossed the line with her. How far did he go? *She'll never tell me.*

"I SPOKE TO NURSE LAURA. YOU PULLED THE wrong plug, Bryn," Jasper said. "You didn't kill him. When you two left the room, he was still alive."

Jasper said that Nurse Laura's granddaughter had been abused by Randolph. She had been poisoning him gradually, and that was the reason our father never recovered. Dr. Carlisle was aware of her actions and was an accomplice to them. The doctor also regularly cheated on his wife, and that was how he fell into Julia's web. She seduced him, and on one drunken, lustful night, got him to admit that Nurse Laura killed Randolph.

"And he mentioned that one of you pulled the wrong plug, so the family never suspected he'd been poisoned. But I had learned post-autopsy. I thought you poisoned him, Bryn. I never suspected Laura. That was one I missed," Jasper said then rubbed his top lip, frowning as if he was disappointed with himself. "Nevertheless, Julia twisted the facts for her benefit. Carlisle was paying her to keep quiet, and Boomer paid her for proof of the false accusation she made against the two of you."

Jasper was spot-on about convincing Penina to take Julia's money. Julia would do anything to remain wealthy, and that meant getting rid of the competition. As far as Julia was concerned, Penina would have to eat or be eaten.

"But what about the cousin she was supposed to marry, Jasper? The guy who owned the sports team?"

"Brandon Valentine?" Jasper asked.

"Is that his name?"

Jasper nodded. "He caught her embezzling money out of his business accounts but couldn't prove it because she's so slick."

Bryn sniffed. "But you can prove it, can't you Ace?"

Jasper smiled big. "You better believe it. And we'll use it when we need it."

WHEN OUR MEETING ENDED, I CALLED PENINA. SHE was on a private airplane with Greg Carroll, on the way to see her mother in Madison, Wisconsin. Next, I placed a call to Nestor, the investigator I hired to assist Penina's aunt's investigator. He gave me the report on Mary Ross. It had been a long time since I flew in one of the family's fleet of aircrafts, but I booked a flight, and not long after, I was on my way to get my woman.

Seventeen

PENINA ROSS

The airplane raced down the runway, pinning us to our seats. Even as we climbed into the sky, Greg and I sustained our stare down. He was wrong to gloat about a perceived blip in my relationship with Asher. Asher would understand that I had to leave. I would see my mother, and that would suffice. *One look —that's all.*

"Don't worry. I'm on your side, not his," he said finally.

I rolled my eyes. "There are no sides. Asher and I are on one side, together, the same side."

"So, what's going on, anyway? What's up with your mother?"

A wave of nausea rolled through my stomach, and I pressed a hand over my navel. I stared into Greg's eyes, deliberating whether I should share or not. A line would be crossed if I chose to do it. However, there was no need to fool myself. I'd lost all credibility as Greg's doctor the moment I chose to drive his Hummer and ride in his airplane. My judgment was off, and I wondered why.

I shook my head and gazed out the window. It was still light out, but clouds were thick beneath the aircraft. "It's personal."

"Oh, come on, Penina. We're friends, aren't we?"

"You're my patient."

"I *was* your patient. You healed me."

I turned to see how he looked when he said such a thing. His grin was stretched from ear to ear.

Wanting to say it, I sighed. I wanted to get it off my chest. "My mother has changed her name, remarried, and started a brand-new family."

Greg's features expanded. "Wow, that's awful."

I went on to tell him about my upbringing and how my mom had dragged me from one rat- and roach-infested hovel to the next—and in front of the occasional letch, who hoped my mom was willing to sell me for her next hit.

"She never would've done that. At least that's one thing I'm grateful to her for."

Then I told him about how I came to be. As a runaway, Mary was sexually abused by a man named Arthur Valentine.

"*The* Arthur Valentine? The one who's serving time for raping and sexually exploiting little girls for over three decades?"

I was shocked that he knew about the notorious Arthur Valentine and when I hadn't until a few days ago. I'd been spending far too much time in a hospital, detached from anything outside the world of medicine. But finally, I was no longer a resident. Soon, and as early as the next day, I would be joining the real world again. I would make it a point to learn all there was to know about society.

"Yes," I said with a sigh. "That guy."

"Wow," he said, rubbing his chin. "That's heavy."

"Tell me about it." I let my head fall back as I groaned. "But let's stop talking about the past and discuss the future."

He smirked. "Our future?"

I sniffed, rolling my eyes. "Sort of. Monday morning, I'll call the Voyagers' front office and ask—"

His hands shot up. "Hold up there. You're talking about me. I'm talking about you. What are you going to do when you see your mother?"

Suddenly, I felt numb inside. "Nothing. I'm just going to look at her and leave." The hardness of my heart made my ears burn.

"Just a look?"

I nodded. "I want to see it all—the house, the kids, the husband, the minivan, all of it."

Greg snorted. "You're envisioning a utopia, huh?"

The answer was yes, but I didn't want to admit it, because I was sure he wouldn't understand why I knew that to be true, so I shrugged.

Greg readjusted in his seat and stretched his massive neck from left to right. "The first time I was hit hard, playing football, I was eleven. A big kid named Webber Smith nailed me good. My helmet flew off, and when my head slammed into the ground, I saw a white light and felt nothing. I thought I was dead, but then everything came into focus. Pain was pounding in my head, blood gushing from my nose.

"My dad was one of the assistant coaches. He asked, 'You okay?' That look in his eyes—" Greg gazed at me, but his eyes were unfocused. "I knew what to say to make him proud of me. And I wasn't going to have him ashamed of me. I nodded. He slapped me on the back and told them to clean me up, and somehow, I finished that game."

Riveted by his account, I gulped.

Greg cleared his throat. "That night, I felt death trying to take me. But I'd take a hit from Hercules to get an 'atta boy' from my father.

"In high school, the hits got harder. College, they got worse. And now, each one feels possibly life ending. I hated football then and even more now. Training starts the end of next month, and I'm dreading it. My dad is going to be calling the front office, asking for favors though. Asking about my training plan. You know who he is, don't you?"

I shook my head. "I don't know who anyone is. I spend too much time in a hospital." I smiled tightly, thinking of how pathetic that sounded.

"Randy Carroll, head coach of the Miami Sun Lords."

He paused to see if that name rang a bell. I shook my head again because it didn't.

"You know who I'd be if I wasn't trying to make Randy happy? A farmer. I like making crops grow.

They call me the wall of steel. But this body"—he slapped himself on one shoulder and the other, and the sound of muscle being smacked filled the air— "it's not mine. It's heavy, and I can't stand it. That's why I take whatever they give me. Those supplements that messed with my brain, they bulk me up. I'm telling you this, Penina, because if you think being raised by two parents is the litmus test for having a happy, normal life, then you're not as smart as I thought you were."

I could tell Greg was rattled by what he had shared with me in the same way I had been after recounting my childhood.

I swallowed to moisten my tight throat. "I know that," I whispered. "Sometimes when I'm wallowing in self-pity, I forget it."

We smiled gently at each other as the pilot announced that we should prepare for landing in ten minutes. I almost felt like a fool for being in Madison, Wisconsin, stalking Lizzie Thompson, who used to be Mary Ross.

"It's not self-pity," Greg said. "It's just how it is. You went through it. I went through it. And that's it."

I nodded. "You're really a smart guy. You know that?"

He winked. "That's why I like smart girls."

I sniffed, shaking my head. The guy was relentless.

"Think about it," he continued. "You and me in bed on a Sunday afternoon, having long conversations about deep stuff, and screwing like rabbits." All his teeth showed when he smiled. They were all white and pristine. He took very good care of them.

"Okay, I'll think about it." I closed my eyes. I really gave it a go, picturing the shower from that morning. I saw myself lying on the bench, two strong arms curled around my thighs. The biceps weren't extra large, but they were muscular. Wet skin against skin. The softness, heat, stimulation against my clit. The tingling in my inner thighs. Extreme pleasure expanding through me. I whimpered and sucked air. One sensation built on top of the next, bringing me to a full blast of orgasm. And when I looked up, steadying my breast, gazing into the eyes of the one who made me feel that way, I saw a color as blue as the Caribbean Ocean as seen in a travel brochure and just as alluring.

"I love him," I said finally. "I love his face, his voice, his gait, his smell, his intensity, the way he handles a scalpel—that's sexy. He's fun. We like to dance and laugh together. He's promising. When I think of loving Asher Blackstone, I can give it all up for an apple farm and babies." I opened my eyes again. "I love him."

Greg cleared his throat. "Then he's a lucky man," he whispered.

Eighteen

PENINA ROSS

Greg and I were in a rented SUV. I had never gone from an airplane to a rented car so fast in my life. When we'd disembarked, we walked down the ramp into a private terminal and out the door. Since we had no luggage, we went straight to the big black Suburban that was waiting for us.

I looked up at the sky before we got in. The clouds were thick, gray, and foreboding. Streaks of lightning raced through the air, and I jumped when I heard a boom. The dreariness added to the fact that I felt as if I were living in the world of a video game or a bad futuristic film in which everyone died in the end. What was happening didn't feel real at all.

Greg asked me to program the address into the navigational system. He turned the air conditioning on full blast. Even though the evening was dark, it was hot and muggy too. As soon as the address was in and Greg pulled away from the curb, the heavens opened, and it started to pour. Water crashing down onto the roof intermingled with the pop music that Greg turned up way too loud for my taste.

I bit down on my back teeth to keep my chin from trembling. Watching the trees as we passed them by, I wondered what in the hell I was thinking. It wasn't too late to abandon my mission. It seemed Greg had quit flirting after I passionately revealed how much I loved Asher. He was quiet, and I liked not having to converse with him or anyone else at the moment.

Taking the opportunity to bargain with myself, I decided that all I needed to see was the house—or maybe only her face. I didn't want to see the kids or her respectable husband. *Is she still messed up?*

Suddenly, the music was turned off. "So, how are you feeling?" Greg asked.

Hugging myself tight, I turned to him. His gaze was distant, yet he seemed to be searching for something in my expression—something lost.

"Scared," I mumbled.

"We can go get a hotel room, and you can do this tomorrow."

"No," I said emphatically. "I have to be back in New Orleans by tonight." I wanted to call Asher again, but I also didn't want to hear how angry my decision had made him. I wasn't ready to admit I was wrong for taking off without thinking it through. And with Greg Carroll too.

"You do see the weather, don't you?"

"Yeah. What about it?" I asked, clutching my stomach.

He glanced at me then did a double take. "Are you okay?"

The navigation system told Greg to take a right on Cherry Street. I remembered the address by heart—1298 Cherry Street. We were near.

I opened my mouth to answer him but found that I couldn't breathe—no matter how hard I tried, I just couldn't.

"Penina?" he asked, trying to watch the road and me.

I clutched my throat. "Pull over," I strained to say, tugging at my shirt and ripping the buttons open. I needed air, fresher than what was coming out of the vents.

"Okay, okay, okay," Greg said, sounding panicked.

As soon as I could feel the car was no longer in motion, I shoved open the door. Falling onto my knees on a stranger's lawn, I gasped for air. But the humidity and heat made my breathing worse. My head was spinning, and my body was tense. I thought I might die.

It didn't take long for Greg to be right by my side, coaching me to calm down and breathe. I tried to come to the awareness that I was having a panic attack so that I could stop myself. The next thing I knew, I broke down sobbing.

"I can't," I kept repeating. "I can't see her."

"You don't have to," Greg said, holding me tight. "We can get back in the car, get back on the airplane, and get the hell back to New Orleans. You like that?" He looked me straight in the eyes, trying to get me to hold eye contact with him.

Calm yourself, Penina.

I didn't nod or say yes, because I didn't know if I truly wanted to abandon my mission. Something inside me still had to see her.

"Could we sit for a moment?" I asked.

Just then, lightning streaked through the sky as

thunder boomed. I could finally feel the wet grass soaking through my pants.

I shot to my feet. "Maybe not."

Perhaps the thunder and the discomfort from being wet were signs that I should get as far away from Cherry Street as possible.

———

It was raining cats and dogs. I sat in the seat, trying to compose myself as Greg called the charter service. After a lot of exclamation and groaning, Greg informed me that the charter service wouldn't be able to clear our flight back to New Orleans because of weather conditions.

I fought the urge to shiver, holding myself tight. We were still on Cherry Street, not very far from my mother's house. I had questions but was too defeated to ask them.

"The service booked us a room at the Baywater Hotel," he said. "The presidential suite was all they had available."

Finally, I sprang to life. "One room? Then let's stay at another hotel."

"No, Penina. I'm Greg Carroll. I'm staying at the Baywater, and so are you."

I realized when Greg whipped a U-turn and zoomed down the street that there was a battle to be had, but I had no fight in me. Or maybe I didn't want to insist he drop me off at the airport so I could book the first commercial flight I could find back to New Orleans. If we remained in town, then I could return to Cherry Street, maybe later that night or early in the morning. Perhaps I would see her wrangle the kids into the car before they went off to church. Mom had never been religious, but she lived in a neighborhood of cozy, custom-built houses with pointed gables, aged trees, healthy lawns, and long driveways with cars big enough for full families. Those people went to church. It was what their parents had done and their parents before them.

On the way to the hotel, Greg seemed to regret speaking to me so harshly. He kept commenting on the bright side of staying at the Baywater Hotel, like the good food and how comfortable the beds were. He said he would give up the master and sleep on the pullout in the living room. I neglected to ask if he had stayed there before, feeling as if he was pulling all those upsides out of his ass.

But I couldn't get the words on the green street sign out of my head.

Cherry Street.
Cherry Street.
Cherry Street.

It was after eight o'clock, and I hadn't had a bite to eat since the turkey and cheese sandwich on the airplane. I was famished and dog-tired when we walked into the hotel room. It was definitely a stunner, tastefully decorated and modern. The comfy sofa was aqua and made of velour, and two cloth-upholstered sitting chairs faced each other, all on top of a dark hardwood floor. The décor was supposed to put me at ease, and it did. I was able to relax a hair, and I felt the void of not speaking to Asher since before takeoff. If he had attempted to call me, he wouldn't have reached me because my cellphone was still in airplane mode.

I flopped onto the sofa and put my phone in regular-use mode. It buzzed, dinged, chimed, and rang. It was Asher. His ears must've been burning.

I hit the answer button. "Asher? Hello."

"Where are you?" Even though he sounded as calm as a serene lake, I could tell he was seething.

Greg came out of the bathroom and clapped

loudly. "This hotel room is nice. Come on, let's go eat, beautiful."

I closed my eyes, feeling dread. I had no doubt Asher had heard all of what he had said. And I wasn't so sure what Greg had done was unintentional. I'd wanted to be the one to explain all that had happened before saying, *And now we're in a hotel room together, but I'm sleeping in the bed, and he's on the sofa.*

"Give him the phone," Asher said in the same overly composed voice.

"Huh?" I asked, confused about why he would want to speak to Greg.

"Give Greg Carroll the goddamn phone." He spoke slowly and concisely.

I turned to see Greg standing in front of the alcove that led to the front door, looking bright-eyed, bushy-tailed, and ready to chow down on a feast.

"Come on. I'm a big boy. I gotta eat. Let's go." He sounded as if he were wrangling the troops.

I quickly got up, holding my cell phone out for him to take. "Um, here."

He frowned but took the phone. "What do you want, Sparrow? Oh, I mean Blackstone?"

I was right—he did know Asher was on the phone.

Greg's frown intensified as he listened. Then he sniffed bitterly and handed my device back to me. "Let's go." He turned and stomped out of the hotel room.

"You're at the Baywater, and you're coming downstairs?" Asher asked.

"Um, yeah, how did you—"

He hung up.

My mouth remained stuck open as I joined Greg in the hallway. "What did he say to you?" I asked.

"Forget him. If he snoozes, he loses."

"Loses what?"

"Let's just get food. I'm hungry, Penina. And your guy just pissed me off. I have to eat, or I'll rip his head off."

I jerked my head back as his heavy steps resonated through the hallway. I wasn't afraid of an angry Greg, but I was surprised by his temper. He'd been quite amicable until then.

I needed to think, to take a shower, to stop

seeing that street sign in my head, and to have a longer conversation with Asher. But I was starving too. Food would help me sort out my confusion.

So I sighed and followed Greg into the elevator. I would eat first then go to the front desk and ask if they definitely had no other rooms for the night. By the way Greg was looking at me, eyes narrowed but glistening with lust, I had been a fool to ever believe him.

Greg pressed the down button, and the elevator doors closed.

"I would still like a chance with you," he said once we were enclosed in the small space.

I gulped, watching him without blinking. "I thought we were becoming friends." I barely had enough breath to say that.

When he snorted brusquely, I knew it was because he found my reply patronizing.

"You know who I am, right?" he asked.

I frowned, confused. "What does who you are have to do with this moment?"

He sneered. "I'm Greg Carroll. I've never been turned down, not even by hotter chicks than you."

Whoa. I jerked my head back, pretty sure he'd just shown me how insincere he truly was. His comment was designed to knock me down a peg or two as well, but it hadn't. I didn't give a damn about how "hot" I was to him.

"Great. Then by all means, go pursue those hotter chicks, you jerk," I snapped.

It looked like he was going to reach out to touch me, but he pulled back. "I'm sorry for that, Penina. I …"

The doors slid open, and we peered into the pale-blue eyes of Asher Blackstone.

Nineteen

〜

PENINA ROSS

The first thing Asher said was that both of us had to go with him because our flight was waiting.

Greg snarled. "I'm not going anywhere with you."

"Jerry Cartwright is expecting you in his office first thing in the morning. I was being generous, letting you ride in my aircraft. But I don't care what you do." He narrowed his eyes at me. "Penina, you're coming with me."

I nodded. Asher wasn't going to receive an ounce of pushback from me. I could smell him from where I stood. The scent coming off him was not cologne, as Greg had insisted. No, it was freshly laundered clothes intermixed with his citrus and mint soap. The scent was mouthwatering. I wanted to eat him alive. But it was crystal clear that Asher was pissed off at me. He didn't hug me or touch me, and he barely looked at me.

Once Cartwright's name had been mentioned, it was as if Greg turned into an obedient robot. Asher would not let me out of his sight, though, as we went upstairs and retrieved what little we had brought with us. I only had my handy tote bag in which I carried all my stuff, from toothpaste to tampons.

Greg drove the rental car back to the airport, and I rode in a hired car with Asher. Still, he didn't say a word until I asked if he was going to speak to me.

"What do you want me to say, Penina?"

"Don't you want to know how it went?"

"I know how it went. You didn't see your mother."

My chest felt tight. "How do you know?"

"If you were there, Penina, then I would've found you at her home."

My mouth fell open. "You went to her house?"

"Yes."

"Did you see her?"

"Yes."

I had no idea what to say, even though I had a million questions to ask about her.

"She didn't know who I was, though." Finally, he looked at me. "You should've waited. We could've come together and arranged a more appropriate meeting between the two of you."

"Did you tell her who you were?" I asked.

His eyes narrowed a pinch more. I could tell he was annoyed by me not addressing his last remark. There was nothing to say other than that he was right. I should've waited for him.

"No, I didn't tell her who I was." His tone was as icy as the energy he was filling the car with.

"And I know, Asher. Okay. I should've waited for you, but I wasn't thinking clearly."

"No, you were not."

I heaved a sigh. *Does he want me to fall on my sword? Gouge my eyes out? Kiss his ring? Cry at his feet?* Well, I was not going to do any of those things, even though deep down inside, the fear of losing him made me want to do whatever it took to remain on his good side.

"I'm sorry, okay?" Then I shook my head. *Why am I apologizing to him?* He wasn't my husband. Also, the last time I saw him, he was walking off with his ex-girlfriend. "But you know, Asher, I don't owe you an apology."

"I know you don't," he said, to my surprise. "Not yet, at least."

My entire face collapsed into a severe frown. "What do you mean by 'not yet'?"

"When I marry you, I'll be your husband, and you'll know to think twice before you go running off with Greg Carroll."

I gulped, absorbing the part about marrying me. *Is Asher proposing to me? Would I say yes if he was? Should I ask him if that's what that was? A proposal? No, Penina. Don't ask.*

Instead, I turned to look out the window and watched the landscape roll by, though I didn't really see anything at all, and allowed what was last spoken the opportunity to fizzle away into the vacuum of inconsequence.

"You mentioned Jerry Cartwright," I said finally.

"What about him?"

I turned to face his burning blue eyes, and they nearly set my heart on fire. "The organization already knows how the supplements they gave him affected his memory?"

"Yes, they do."

My shoulders curled forward. "I should've—"

"Don't beat yourself up, Penina. What's done is done."

I sighed briskly, pressing my lips together, annoyed by the way he was icing me out. "So we're not on good terms right now, are we?"

"Damn it!" he shouted, wringing his hands.

I leaned away from him. "What the hell, Asher?"

"He lied to you, Penina. Every step of the way. And you put yourself in a dangerous situation. He's bigger than you. And if he wanted to have you, there was no way you could stop him. When a guy goes to those lengths to get you alone, he won't stop until he gets what he wants. So don't ever do that again. Understand?"

I was speechless. Part of me wanted to defend Greg and the budding friendship I'd thought we were building. The other part seriously heeded his warning. *You snooze, you lose.* That was what Greg had said. *What would he have done when I got into the shower naked?* I would've locked the door, of course. I would've locked the room door when I went to bed as well. But my plans to keep myself safe said something about how much I hadn't truly trusted Greg. That look in his eyes when we were in the elevator said it all. He was a man on the hunt. Asher had ruined his endeavor to bed me. *Dang it. What was I thinking?*

"I understand," I was forced to say to the man who might one day be my husband if that indeed was what he'd meant by his perplexing comment.

He nodded graciously. "Thank you. And as far as treating your patient goes, you did exemplary work, Dr. Ross."

Asher told me three other team members had reported the same symptoms as Greg. Another had been involved in a car accident late that afternoon. While he was driving, he had forgotten where he was and what he was doing. Other than whiplash, he was okay. But he was also taking the supplements.

"Wow," I said.

"Yes. Team management is grateful for our efforts, which is why we'll be working together in the future. We're going to have an informal in-flight meeting on the way back."

His pause and the penetrating way that he looked at me made me nervous.

"What?" I asked.

"Julia will be part of that call."

My mouth fell open, then I had to remind myself to breathe.

FINALLY, WE MADE IT TO THE AIRPORT. ASHER opened my door and took my bag and my hand, and we walked to the terminal for private flights. I was glad we'd finally made skin-on-skin contact, even if it was just our hands. That meant he was less angry with me.

Greg met us at the gate shortly after we arrived. His grimace moved from Asher and me holding hands to my bag hanging from my boyfriend's shoulder. He cut his eyes away from us and stomped down the ramp to board the airplane. Asher muttered something about Greg not having the class to wait until the owner of the aircraft boarded first. I didn't have to be a brain surgeon to grasp that they hated each other, but I refused to believe I was the reason why. No way. Their egos were the culprits.

The inside of Asher's airplane was as roomy as a regular 747. It was something I'd thought I would never see or experience in real life. The setup reminded me of the penthouse. It had two expensive-looking white sofas, one on each side of the cabin. On a platform was a large table with four reclining chairs around it, two on each side. But there were so many little details too, like appropriately placed smaller tables and single sitting benches.

Greg had taken a seat on one of two large chairs set in the front of the aircraft. Asher and I sat at the table. There were two flight attendants, both friendly and pretty and happy to flirt back with Greg.

"Sorry, Mr. Carroll. Alcohol will not be served on this flight," said the flight attendant who'd asked what he would like to drink.

"What the hell, Blackstone!" Greg boomed. "A fancy airplane with no drinks."

Asher pretended not to hear him as he continued programming a panel on the table. "Once we're in the air, you should come over here and join the meeting, Carroll."

"What meeting?" Greg asked.

"The one Jerry's going to be in."

Greg didn't respond, but it was clear he understood where he would be sitting once Jerry was on the line. I recalled what Greg had revealed to me about his father as Asher continued doing whatever he was doing to prepare for the in-flight call. It was as if the fastest way to convince Greg to comply was to mention Jerry. And I was sure Asher knew it, which was why it was the second time he'd used Jerry to get Greg to do what he needed him to do.

The flight attendant asked what I would like to drink while staring at Asher, who was paying no attention to her whatsoever.

I wanted to snap my fingers and say, "Hey, eyes on me, not him."

"She'll have sparkling water with lime," Asher said without looking at either of us.

Greg scoffed. I assumed it was his reaction to Asher ordering for me.

"Thank you, and you, sir?" she asked.

"Just dinner," he said.

"And hot tea, Earl Grey, with a little milk and honey. He'll have that." I'd heard him place that order at the café in the hospital between surgeries on several occasions.

Finally, he smiled at me.

We stared at each other. My heart beat like crazy. Then his eyes narrowed just a pinch before he went back to programming the console.

If we were alone, I would've asked why he was being so distant. However, I didn't want Greg to know things were tense between us. Thank good-ness the pilot announced we were on our way to the runway. The flight attendants came into the cabin to serve our drinks and make sure we were buckled up. The one with dark hair and red lipstick made eyes at Greg. As I watched her, I felt eyes on me. I quickly looked at Asher, who was glaring back at me.

My lips parted. I wanted to explain that I wasn't staring because I was jealous. I was simply marking an observation in my head. But Asher had turned away before I could try to explain.

Then we were speeding down the runway and climbing to altitude. Once we were settled, the flight attendants served dinner, beef tenderloin with Yukon Gold potato puree, glazed carrots, and a variety of freshly baked breads. Asher hardly touched his meal, while Greg and I devoured ours. We'd had an eventful day.

After fiddling with the controls on the table, Asher made a call to Chief Brown. It was just the two of them, and they were on together for a while. Mostly, Asher said things like "Yes," "No," or "Check that." He was good at having a private conversation with others in the room.

Greg flirted with the stewardess named Willow,

asking her where she was from and whether she had a boyfriend and all sorts of surface questions to keep her talking. I tuned him out, though. I was more interested in trying to decode Asher and Si's conversation. It was difficult to do, and so far, I hadn't been able to pin anything they said together to help me figure out what they were talking about.

Willow and Mina, the other flight attendant, collected our plates. Asher asked them to hold off on dessert, then announced we were ready to begin the call.

"You're not going to eat?" I asked.

His eyes smoldered when he said, "Later."

I melted into my seat. *Was that a double entendre?* I hoped so.

"What's that perfume you're wearing, sexy? It's the best thing I've smelled all day," Greg said to Willow.

"Oh, I'm not wearing perfume," she crooned. "It's against the rules."

"Ooh, then that's your natural scent. Tasty."

I snarled at Greg and the show he was putting on. Wow, after all that personal stuff he'd shared about his father and never loving football, I'd thought he had a heart. What a manipulative jerk.

When I turned, Asher was staring at me again. I

wished he would say something and stop glaring at me as if he was chastising me for paying attention to Greg.

"Willow, please leave us. We're starting the meeting," Asher said.

"Yes, Mr. Blackstone," she said like an obedient flight attendant who got paid a lot of money to remain professional.

Greg held out his hand for her to take. Willow's face was beet red. She hesitated but put her hand on top of Greg's. The thing was that it was her job to make him feel comfortable, and he was crossing many lines. I glared at Asher, on the verge of demanding he put an end to Greg's harassment.

"That'll be all Willow. Leave, please, now," Asher restated.

Willow snatched her hand out of Greg's grasp and scurried into an area where I supposed the kitchen was.

Greg jumped to his feet, glaring at Asher.

Asher didn't flinch. "Stop harassing my flight attendants, and get over here. We're starting."

"Dr. Ross, can you hear me?" Chief Brown asked.

I snapped to attention. "Yes, sir."

And again, Asher gave me an odd look.

"What?" I blurted out. I had no restraint. I was tired. He wasn't telling me why he was tossing me the cross looks, but they were annoying as hell.

Asher shrugged. "Nothing," he said calmly.

"Sounds like trouble in paradise to me," a feathery female's voice said.

I stiffened. It had to be Julia Valentine.

"Greg, you there?" a man with a thick Southern accent asked.

"I'm here, Coach," Greg called as he rushed over and dropped into the seat directly across from Asher.

"Why didn't you tell us about your memory issues, kid?"

I sniffed. *Kid?*

Asher gave me the side-eye as Greg's eyes widened in panic as he looked at me.

I cleared my throat. "Um, we didn't want to alarm anyone," I said, refusing to see how Asher was reacting to my covering for Greg. The guy might have been treating me as if he were a heart-broken teenaged boy, but he was still my patient.

"I understand, but—" Jerry said.

"We know each other through mutual friends. He just came in this morning because I was at the hospital. He wasn't feeling well. So we assembled a team and ran some tests," I said, keeping my attention on the sound modulator on the console.

"I see …" Jerry said. I was certain he hadn't bought my BS excuse. There were a lot of gaps in my cover.

"Anyway, whatever, it happened, and it turned out great for the hospital and your organization, Mr. Cartwright," Julia said.

"Well, as I said, we take brain injuries seriously," Cartwright said.

His last statement was an indication of what he was worried about. All the league wanted was more reports on brain injuries. We'd discussed CTE in one of our seminars the previous year. One thing we'd agreed upon was there would be no public ramifications for the rampant condition discovered in players. People didn't give a damn. They were like the spectators in the Roman Colosseum, watching the gladiators tear each other apart. Who cared if they killed each other and themselves? Just entertain us, please.

"I'm sure you do." Julia sounded desperate to remind everyone that she was an integral part of the conversation.

"Right," Jerry said rather dismissively. "We dodged a bullet. And I shoved a big foot in our health advisors' asses about giving that poison to our players. Lots of them have been out of sorts for a while. If it weren't for you, Greg, we could've lost more than half our team before training camp starts. And that's why Merle is here with me."

Greg's eyes grew super wide. Merle must've been a big deal. Asher, on the other hand, nodded continuously.

"We're happy you can join us, Mr. Barnes," Chief Brown said just as Julia started to say something.

"Call me Merle."

"Merle, we're very excited about our future partnership in our sports medicine wing."

"I heard the Expansive Brain Health Institute will also have a division at the hospital."

"Yes, indeed," the chief said.

"We were thinking maybe we might have a media event," Julia said.

"Well, not yet. We have to let this supplement debacle blow over first."

Asher scooted to the edge of his seat. "Merle, Asher Blackstone here. There's no need for you to worry about any negative impact. We have it all under control."

"Mr. Blackstone," Merle said excitedly. "It's an

honor to be talking to you, and anything you need from us, we're ready and able to assist you."

"I appreciate that, Merle."

"And the brilliant doctor who saved our asses, is she with you?"

Asher looked at me and nodded.

"Yes, sir, I'm here."

"I would like to thank you for persevering to the end."

"Well …" Julia's voice came in loud and clear. "Dr. Ross didn't inform administration of her findings before traipsing off to God knows where. But that's an internal matter."

Asher's frown was so severe that it looked like he was chewing on lemons. It remained deathly silent for a few beats.

Julia went on to give the logistics of a future meeting that was planned, including time and participants, then she was released from the call. We all said our final goodbyes before Asher got up and went into a private space to finish the rest of the call with the chief.

Once Greg and I were alone, he stared daggers at me. There was no way I was going to shrink away from that look on his face, so I did the same.

After a moment, he sniffed bitterly and got up,

and just as if he'd rung a bell, Willow came out, and he resumed flirting with her.

By the time he got to the part where he asked her out to dinner the next time she was in town, I was dozing off. When my eyes opened again, the airplane was parked at the terminal, and Asher was calling my name while gently shaking me awake.

I WAS SURPRISED THAT GREG WAS KEEPING STRIDE with us. I'd thought he would storm off on his own, but he stayed close. Asher's pinched expression was a clue that he was bothered by it. Once we were on the sidewalk in the arrivals pick-up area, Greg pointed at Asher.

"You can give her the bag back. Since she rode here with me, I'll take her back to the hospital," Greg blurted out, looking as angry as a bull.

Asher put his arm around my shoulder. "Back off, asshole."

Greg sneered like a schoolyard bully. "What are you going to do, pretty boy?"

Asher removed his hand and stepped away to put distance between him and me. My heart pounded so hard that the sound resonated in my ears. *What the hell is happening? Are two fully grown and professional men about to fight?*

"You guys, stop it. Go home, Greg!" I yelled. "I'm leaving with Asher."

"What are you going to do?" Greg asked, his attention focused on Asher. It was as if he hadn't heard or couldn't absorb a word I had said.

I wondered if the stage-one CTE was making Greg more aggressive than the average person. I was also worried about Asher. He was by no means scrawny, but he had less than half the body mass of Greg. I searched up and down the walkway, looking for any signs of security.

"Back off, buddy," Asher said in a tone that made me wonder if I was more worried about Greg taking his head off than he was. Asher stood his ground, showing no signs of backing down from whatever fight Greg wanted to have.

Then, striking like lightning, Greg threw a punch at Asher. And like a superhero in a big-screen movie, Asher dodged Greg's fist. Greg swung again, and Asher easily avoided him again.

I was either unable to yell for help or unable to decide if I should.

"Be sure you want to finish what you're starting." The calm in Asher's voice was further indication of his impeccable control.

Asher stood steady, not moving a muscle. His eye contact was firm. He'd already easily evaded powerful blows that could've put his lights out.

Greg's eyes were glazed over as if he acknowledged for a fraction of a second that Asher might have been more of a skilled fighter than he appeared to be. He opened his mouth then closed it, and without another word, he turned and padded down the walkway. People watched, snapping cell phone pictures of all of us.

Asher took me by my hand. "Let's get the hell out of here."

I nodded gently and walked beside him. With all the excitement, I hadn't seen Kirk parked nearby. Asher held the door open, and I slid into the back seat. He got in after me.

We were alone again, and we had so much to talk about.

"I'm sorry," I said to break the ice.

"No need to continue apologizing, Penina."

His icy tone worried me. *Has he lost all trust in me?*

I sighed, giving in to defeat. "Okay." My sinuses grew tight as I chose to face away from him. If our relationship was beyond repair, then so be it.

Frankly, I thought there was a conversation we should have, but I had no idea how to start it. Mature, adult relationships had always been beyond my grasp.

"You were staying in a hotel room with him," Asher said finally.

I whipped my head around to face him again, relieved he spoke. "He said there were no rooms."

His frown intensified. "Did you bother to check?"

I shook my ahead, ashamed that I hadn't.

"Have you done some soul searching, Penina?"

My eyebrows were pinched. "Meaning?"

"Did you want to be in a hotel room with him? Did you want to be seduced into sex with him?"

"No." My tone was firm. "That was not what I wanted, Asher. I was not in my right mind." I shook my hands emphatically. "Plus, he was nice. He was being a friend."

His Adam's apple bobbed as he gulped. The fact that he hadn't looked away from me was a good sign.

"Listen, there was no part of me that was physically or sexually attracted to Greg. And yes, I should've gone down to the front desk to see if there were other rooms. And I was going to do that after dinner. And I would've taken a commercial flight back to New Orleans. I wanted to do that, too, but I also wanted to stay in Wisconsin, just in case I found the nerve to follow through and see my mother. You know, maybe I'm not ready for a relationship. Maybe I'm just not good at it. I'm not able to do it without screwing it up."

Is that disappointment in his eyes? I refused to look away from his probing gaze. I wanted him to find whatever he was searching for inside me.

After a few more moments, he turned to stare straight ahead.

"When I was with Julia, she used other men to make me jealous," he said finally.

My chest caved in as I sighed. *Am I like her?* I knew better than to believe that nature was stronger than nurture. Julia's brain and my brain had absorbed and adapted to different stimuli, so surely, I couldn't have ended up like her.

"But I wasn't trying to make you jealous, Asher. That was not my intention."

He gulped again. "Did he touch you?"

I had to look away to remember.

"Penina. That should've been a hard no."

"Well …" I shook my hands, panicky. "When I

made him stop the car and I fell on someone's lawn to catch my breath, I cried, and he consoled me."

He scratched the side of his face as he watched me with his customary probing stare.

"I didn't know that," he whispered.

"I didn't tell you. You didn't ask, either."

Slowly, with the same sort of control he'd exhibited during the altercation with Greg, Asher took in a deep breath and released it. We stared at each other, trapped in a moment of confusion.

"I'm only human, Asher. A flawed human being who can be susceptible to being suckered."

"Don't," he said.

My eyebrows pulled together.

"Don't apologize again. I know you're sorry. And so am I."

Twenty

PENINA ROSS

When he said he was sorry, I felt as if my whole world came crashing down on me. We didn't say anything else to each other until Kirk stopped in front of my building.

"Thanks for the ride," I said as I grasped the door, refusing to look at his face.

"Don't open the door, Penina. Not while I'm in the car."

I rolled my eyes. Forget him and his chivalry. "That's okay. I got it."

"Babe, no. But I would like for you to pack a suitcase and come stay with me for a while."

I froze, then when I remembered to breathe, I laid a hand against my breastbone. "What?" I asked, turning to face him. I was seriously shocked. I'd thought he was ending our relationship. And the way things were going, I had no desire to fight for us, figuring he wanted a soulless machine who made no mistakes that would hurt him.

His bright eyes glistened in the dark cab. "There's no need for us to be apart."

"You're not breaking up with me?"

"No, Penina," he replied as if that were the silliest thing I'd ever said. "We hit a rough patch. That doesn't mean we break up."

Still, I was confused, and I was sure it showed on my face.

"Stay put," he said then got out of the car and opened my door.

My head felt woozy as I stood. Something was happening inside me. I was undergoing a transformation. We stood inches away from each other, gazing into each other's eyes, our breaths warming the space between us.

"Good night, resident and attending," someone said.

We both whipped our attention toward Jen Lovely, my next-door neighbor, who glared as if she was scolding us.

Asher guided his mouth next to my ear as he took my hand. "Come."

MY LEGS FELT RESTLESS AS WE ENTERED MY apartment. My lightheadedness hadn't left me since we were outside by the car. *Did we just talk through our first major argument, which was brought about by my impulsiveness? Did we resolve it?*

My apartment looked as if a tornado had touched down in it. I always managed to leave it in such a mess before rushing out for my shift. That morning, I had tried on two pairs of pants, and the black slacks that I rejected were draped across the back of the sofa.

"Sorry for the—"

ASHER TUGS ME AGAINST HIS FIRM BODY, AND I TASTE his tongue, feeling it brush fervently against mine. He's hard in several places—chest, thighs, cock. He whispers that I'm soft all over. His strong hands take me by my hips, and he grinds his erection against me. I know what message he's sending. So when he lifts my feet off the ground, I wrap my legs around him and continue indulging in the taste of Asher Blackstone.

Asher carries me through my own apartment. He's not confused about where he should go or how to get there. That becomes even more obvious when I feel my mattress against my back.

"Damn, baby," he mutters then sucks my neck hard and licks it as he nails his cock deep into my slit and rubs it. Then he moans as he tosses his head back and sucks air.

I watch him through my hooded gaze. His face is so sexy when he's turned on, so needy, so lustful. He is the embodiment of the calm before a raging storm. We've been here before. I know what comes next, and my sex jumps with excitement, eager for the action to start.

Asher's rapt attention focuses on my body as he tugs my shoes off then my pants and my panties. Plunk, plunk, cling, swish ... I hear them all land somewhere, making the smallest to the greatest impact.

Asher spreads my knees apart, gazing at my slit as the cold conditioned air presses against it. I squirm, my breathing impatient. He takes so long to make up his mind about what to do to me next. Do I have a preference? I can't think of one. I like it all. Love it all. Want it all.

"Oh, Asher," I finally whine, lifting my pelvis toward him. Choose one already.

Then he pushes my thighs toward me. I push the back of my head against the mattress, bracing myself for it.

"Ah!" I cry.

Wet. Warm. Full. One lick of my clit sends shivers of pleasure through me. More licks, more stimulation. I clamor for less, for more, grabbing the sheets, whimpering.

"Oh, baby, please..." It's so intense.

And as soon as my body tightens and I attempt to free my clit from his tongue, he knows what to do next. "Mm," he moans and whimpers. His tongue works more fervently. I claw at anything I can grasp, but nothing can ease the pleasure.

More.

I can't ...

"Ah!" I cry to the high heavens on explosion. The orgasmic sensation is strong, deep, and lasting. It spreads through me like a desert wind. I forget to breathe as it continues. I can't ...

"Damn!" Asher blurts out.

He lets go of me. He frees me. I curl into a ball as the remains of the orgasm refuse to release me. I hear his belt hit the floor. Then his hands are on my knees again. He spreads them. Skin on skin, I take hold of him. His heaviness secures me to the mattress. His manhood soars through me.

He calls, "Oh, baby. Yes..." And so do I.

The bed bangs, creaks, and knocks.

Our lips melt. He feels so good, stretching me. His cock pumps in and out of my caves. He's so thick, so engorged. My eyes grow as wide as they can possibly go. I'm riding a wave of euphoria.

Then he mutters something indecipherable. It happens rapidly. His large palms grip my butt cheeks. I'm no longer beneath him. I'm on top, digging into the sheets as he shifts me against him fast, and then slow.

"Ah!" I cry as he plugs me deep and fastens his cock deep inside me, then he kisses the side of my face as his mouth searches greedily for mine.

We whimper as we kiss because we can't seem to satiate ourselves. I want him so much. I need him like I need air. I want to swallow his mouth as I take his face in my hands.

"I love you," I whisper.

Those three words are fuel to his fire. He flips me back over, grabs hold of my flimsy backboard, and grunts as he throws all his strength behind his final thrusts.

Wood crashes against plaster. Harder … I tighten around the action so I can feel all of it. Hard … The tickling sensation inside me warns me that a new orgasm is blossoming. I grow tense as I lift my hips so that I can feel it more.

It's coming.

We're coming.

Then we cry out together. Asher tosses his head back as

he shivers and jerks. I quake too. As soon as our pleasure dwindle, he sweeps me up off the mattress and rolls me back on top of him.

EAR AGAINST HIS CHEST, I LOVED LISTENING TO HIS heartbeats and feeling his skin and muscles. I circled my tongue around his nipple and sucked it into my mouth. "Mm," I said as he sucked air. I loved tasting him too.

"I love you too," he whispered in the dim room.

I wanted to put my heart and soul on the table and share something that made me vulnerable.

"I would live on an apple farm with you and have as many kids as you wanted," I said finally.

"Is that so?" he asked, sounding highly inquisitive.

I pressed my lips together, feeling deceitful because I'd omitted telling him that I got the whole notion of an apple farm with kids from Greg.

"You want to live on an apple farm?" he asked.

"Well, no. But I would, only for you."

He chuckled as he ran his large hands down my back then pushed my ass against his cock to keep himself inside me.

"I'm happy to hear it because a day might come when we can't do our jobs like regular people as Blackstones."

I grimaced, sliding my hands up and down his strong torso. "What are you saying?"

"The press can get out of hand. And people in general are fascinated by idols. We become unreal to them. Not even human, and they'll treat us that way."

I smoothed my hand over his chest, indulging in the way his nipple felt against my palm. No wonder men loved tits and nipples so much. I wanted to suck his, too, and make him stiffen and grow hard again so he could pound the hell out of me. But I couldn't get "they'll treat us that way" out of my head. *Does he mean him and me or his family in general?*

Finally, he kissed my forehead. "We should get up and go. We have to get some sleep. We've had a long day."

I raised my head off his chest. "Get up and go? You don't want to sleep here?"

He kissed my forehead again. "No. My bed." He elbowed the mattress. "We almost broke this thing. And I'm not done with you yet."

I gave him a lopsided smile. "I thought you said we had to sleep."

"We're going to sleep for a little while. Then I'm going to do you again, hard, until I get the picture of Greg and you out of my head."

My eyebrows pulled together. "What?"

"I know it's not rational, but it's there." He pointed at his skull. "In there."

ASHER AND I STARED INTO MY NEARLY EMPTY suitcase. He kept reminding me that I didn't have to bring a lot of clothes. The penthouse we would be residing in had been prepared for our arrival.

"It's not the same penthouse that I'm used to?"

He'd said Gina thought she could sell the property to Julia without his permission, which meant the penthouse was currently tied up in a real estate deal. I was shocked the two women were associated in such a way. Gina was Asher's ex-girlfriend too. That explained how Julia had found Asher.

"Gina and Julia are that close?" I asked.

He closed the suitcase and secured the clamps as he said, "No. Julia's never close to anyone. The people she gets to know and everything she does is for her benefit. Remember that and stay the hell away from her."

"Warning heeded for the umpteenth time," I said.

"Good. Keep heeding it." He snatched my suit-case off the bed. "Let's get out of here."

I was still processing the last of his continued warnings about Julia. She was my sister. And at some point, I would have to really mull over that fact—or maybe not. I'd gone so far in life without knowing her. Our blood relation came from a very dark source. Perhaps that was what my mom's running away and changing her identity was all about. Asher had done the same. *Who am I to say they were wrong?* Julia and I had never been sisters and never would be. And that was that, and it was okay.

We walked into the living room, and I stopped at the front door for a final once-over. It was much cleaner. All the stray clothing, pieces of mail that had been on the coffee table, my robe, which had been draped across my office chair, and the one house shoe that had been sitting beside the couch were all put away. I had a strong hunch that I would not be back to the place that I had made home for the past seven years.

"Are you ready?" Asher asked.

Choked up, I nodded.

"Ooh, one more thing," I said and raced to my bedroom.

I opened the closet. Behind rows of shoes I'd never worn, broken umbrellas, and a coat that had dropped off the hanger was the box where I stored important documents. I opened it and shuffled through the pages and envelopes.

"You okay in there?" Asher asked.

I smiled at the envelope my mom used to make me keep with me whenever she went off to do whatever she did to acquire money and drugs. "I am. Got it," I called.

"Got what?" Asher asked.

I showed him the box as I walked back into the living room. "This."

Suddenly, that feeling that I was leaving something behind was gone. I had everything I needed with me and next to me.

"What's that?" he asked.

"Personal documents and stuff."

Asher and I grinned at each other as he opened the door and I passed him. His nearness never failed to make me feel warm and giddy inside. When I stepped into the hallway, so did Kirk. He was coming out of Zara's apartment.

"Kirk," Asher said, seeming surprised to see him.

Kirk's face was as red as a crab's shell. "On my way to the car, boss." He bolted to the stairwell.

Asher set his stunned expression on me. "Really? Those two?"

Pressing my lips together, I nodded.

He grunted thoughtfully and wrapped an arm around my waist as he pulled my suitcase with his other hand, and we were on our way.

───────

THE OTHER PENTHOUSE SUITE WAS LOCATED AT THE Four Seasons Residences. The place was more opulent than the last. It had clean white furniture, contemporary paintings on the walls, and big windows overlooking the lake. Everything looked brand new.

Asher said the residence was one his family owned, and we would be living there until we found a more permanent situation.

"Permanent?" I asked.

We stood in front of the window, staring at the moonlight spreading across the dark water. Asher wrapped me up from behind. He was hard again.

He kissed my exposed shoulder. "I've been thinking. None of what occurred would've happened if you knew for sure we were a duo."

I sniffed. "A duo?"

"Yes, baby. You and me. I want you, Penina. I would propose to you tonight, but I want to give us a little more time to prove to ourselves we belong together."

Frowning, I asked, "What does that even mean?"

Asher searched my expression for several moments. "My family …" His mouth froze as if it was stuck open.

"Your family what?"

He blinked. "Not everyone has the constitution." His hand flew up to rub the back of his neck. "I'm kind of afraid you don't and, if not, what that means for us."

I reached up and carefully seized his nervous hand. When I had it securely in mine, I wove our fingers together. "Try me," I whispered.

He gulped. "Julia's going to be dealt with on Monday."

"What do you mean by 'dealt with'?"

Asher released my hand to wrap his arms around me. He held me close. "My brother Jasper, he's quite severe in the way he deals with people who oppose him ... us." With one eye narrowed, he picked apart my reaction.

I leaned back as far as I could. Asher maintained a vise grip on me, as if he were stopping me from running away. "Is he going to kill her?"

"No," he said, shaking his head vehemently. "Money is how Julia fights. He's going to take it all away from her and ..."

I tilted my head curiously. "And?"

"Give it to another sibling."

"Another sibling?" I mused, then when it became clear which sibling he was referring to, I jerked my head back. "Me?"

"What do you think about that?"

"What do I think about it? I don't know. This is unbelievable stuff you're talking about. Is this what rich people do to each other?"

Asher sniffed. "I can't speak for other rich people, but Blackstones, yes. As I said, my brother's severe. He wouldn't take the action if he saw a better way."

"So, he's going to take all of her money?"

"She used to have more, but he'll take what's left if necessary."

"But she bought the penthouse, so she has a pretty healthy amount."

"Well," he said with a sigh. "Julia's been extorting money from a few ex-employees of ours."

He went on to tell me about a doctor and a nurse who had been assigned to take care of his father. Julia learned that the nurse was the grandmother of one of Randolph's past victims. Then Julia rolled the dice at using that information to her advantage. Her shot paid off. Julia didn't know exactly what the nurse named Laura had done, but the nurse didn't want it getting back to the Blackstones that she had reason to want to see Randolph dead.

Asher and I sat down on the sofa, and he kept his arm around me as I rested my head on his chest while he told me the rest. The story took several turns—his sister Bryn pulling the wrong plug; the nurse poisoning the father for several months; the autopsy results; Randolph being cremated.

"Julia never knew the minute details, yet she was able to extort those who did?" I asked.

"She's smart when it comes to matters like these. She knew they were afraid of something, and that's all she needed to know. But she was the one who told one of my brother's political opponents that Bryn and I murdered our father. He paid her for that information."

"But why would she just make that up?"

Asher sniffed. "She didn't. Julia was having sex with the doctor. She got him inebriated, and he mentioned something about me and Bryn pulling the plug."

I looked up at Asher, and our gazes melted. "Why is your father so loathed anyway?"

"Read the book," he whispered.

My eyelashes fluttered closed. "Soon. Very soon."

I knew what was coming next.

First our lips brush, then the tip of his tongue gently pushes against mine and holds. My eyes open. Our staring intensifies.

Asher's eyebrows flew up and held. "Let's go to bed."

I smirked. "To sleep."

He smirked as well. "That too."

Twenty-One

PENINA ROSS

I wasn't sure if I'd slept. Since the moment we crawled into bed, Asher had been on fire. We made hot passionate love. Then I closed my eyes and dozed off. At a certain point, his hand ran up and down the curve of my waist. I stirred.

"I want to be inside you," he whispered in my ear.

He had slipped inside me many times while I was halfway awake, and I mumbled permission for him to do me again. As usual, when he glided through me, I became more focused on procuring my next orgasm than returning to dreamland.

And when it happened, when my thighs shuddered and I cried out, Asher cupped my tits, squeezing my nipples as he released himself inside me. We stayed that way until we did it again. Then he went down on me, and I had several orgasms. Now, as the light of day poured into the room, I breathed heavily after my body calmed down from another intravaginal orgasm.

I rubbed my forehead. "Have we been totally irresponsible throughout the night?"

Asher was still on top of me. He had told me on several occasions to let him worry about the time. I wasn't going on shift, but I was supposed to meet with Deb to sign some final paperwork. Then I was to report to HR to sign more paperwork that would officially make me the hospital's newest fellow.

Our cell phones weren't in the room with us, so even if my alarm song played, I wouldn't have been able to hear it. I had spent most of my adult life on a time clock. I couldn't relax, but I didn't want to get out of bed either. I loved that he was on top of me and inside me. I relished the fact that his hands had been all over me through the night, even while I slept.

"Okay, babe," I patted him on his back. "We have to finally rise and shine."

He groaned. "I know. But after your meetings, I want you to come home, get in bed, and wait for me."

I chuckled at how utterly insane but fun that sounded. "You mean you want me to walk through that door, take off my clothes, climb in bed, and wait for you?"

Asher's smile added extra light to the room. "In that order, yes."

I tilted my head to feign pondering. I already knew my answer. "Then you'll be my next shift?"

I hummed as his lips visited my earlobe then slid down to my neck, where he whispered, "Night call and all."

I embraced him tighter, hugging him in sweet bliss as I said, "Mm, the sound of that is making me wetter."

"I can feel it," he said, trying to thrust into me with his spent cock. "Just give me a moment." He kept pushing his cock in and out of me, eyes closed, concentrating.

I patted him on the back again. "Asher, no. You're being an awful timekeeper."

He laughed. "I just can't get enough of you." He carefully flipped over onto his back, his heaviness and moist skin abandoning my body.

I pinched my thighs together, enjoying the flickers of the shadow orgasm that occurred when he slipped out of me.

WHEN ASHER SAID THAT I COULD WEAR WHATEVER was in the closets and drawers, I could never have imagined what was in them. The few articles of clothing I'd packed looked like rags next to the high-fashion garments I had access to.

I was also reminded how long it had been since I'd gone shopping. I stood in the walk-in closet, flanked by clothes and shoes, miraculously all in my size. It wasn't coincidence either. *Who did this? How did they know what to buy?* Asher was right—I would have to get used to being a Blackstone if walking into a closet full of racks of clothes displayed as if I were shopping in an upscale boutique was the norm.

I recalled how Julia had been dressed the day before. She'd had on a black skirt suit that fit her so tightly that she looked like a vixen. I was surrounded by prettier suits than the one she'd had on. I opted for a sort of pearl-colored skirt suit and a royal-blue silk camisole. I also put on a pair of black patent-leather Mary Janes. The heels were not too high or too low.

When I saw myself in the standing mirror, I admitted that I looked impeccable. I received even more proof of that when I walked into the kitchen and Asher stopped pouring coffee to stare at me. His reaction was strange. He looked angry yet lustful.

He put down the carafe then walked over and took my hand. Then he put his mouth next to my ear. "Let's go back to bed."

I slipped my hand out of his. "Are you really this blasé about our jobs?"

"I am now," he said before his tongue dove into my mouth and tasted mine.

"By the way," I said against his hungry mouth.

"What?"

His tongue clamored for mine, and I let him have it until I was able to ask, "Who bought all of those clothes?"

"We have people." Asher's hand slipped under my skirt and tugged at the crotch of my panties until his fingers found what they were looking for.

"Ha," I said, gasping as his fingers thrust into me. "Babe. I don't want to be late."

His tongue dove into my mouth, lapping mine several times before he stopped fingering me and took a step back. "Later," he said, pointing at me. "I'm finishing you later."

Allowing my weakened knees to strengthen yet again, I grabbed the counter. "Please do."

―――――――――

In the end, Asher had actually been a great steward of our time. We arrived at the hospital at five minutes to one, and I was supposed to meet Deb at one o'clock. He had other things to do, so we kissed and parted ways. It hadn't occurred to me how off it was that we were meeting on a Sunday until I made it to the conference room. I checked over my shoulder as well, suddenly aware that I hadn't run into anyone either. I wasn't used to that, and I hoped it wouldn't be the new normal. Before leaving for the day, I planned to make sure I said farewell to my team members and all the staff who had been part of my world for the past seven years. I would let them know that we would see one another again on the first of November. Although I was certain they would all mention something about Asher and me being a couple. I would confirm our status as two lovebirds who planned to make a serious go at a long-term relationship. After all, he'd almost proposed to me the previous night. I wasn't hiding us anymore, and neither was he.

Once I had that thought out of the way, I was ready to see Deb. I sighed and opened the door. A blast of streamers and confetti filled the air along with a loud chorus of "Congratulations, Dr. Ross!"

I slapped my hand over my mouth, growing completely still. In front of me were all the people I'd wanted to visit later that day. My eyes watered as I took in Angela, Deb, even Zara, Kevin, and all of my favorite attendings and nurses, including Courtney. And grinning like he was my sun—because he was—was Asher.

I focused solely on his sexy face as I strolled to him, wrapped my arms around him, and planted one sexy kiss on him in front of everyone. We only stopped kissing when a piano started playing. I quickly turned to see what was coming next. Brody, one of the interns, was sitting on a stool, playing the keyboard. The neurosurgery attendings, Dr. Nassim, Dr. Huang, Dr. Kraig, and Dr. Chapman, sang with gusto, "For all the years you've saved our asses, we say thank you! Goodbye, sweet Pen, our darling resident, bright as the moon, who's now a fellow. We'll see you back here soon."

The room filled with applause, and I did something between laughing and crying as I hugged everyone.

There was cake and all my favorite treats from Southern Candymakers and plenty of wine, which I drank because the occasion called for a glass or two. I had a great time reminiscing with my colleagues about the past and our most memorable patients. I decided to call it quits in the middle of my third glass. As usual, the alcohol went right through me, and I had to rush to the ladies' room.

I hadn't heard her come into the restroom, nor had I smelled her overly sweetened perfume. I wished I had. I probably would have stayed in the stall. While looking into the eyes of Julia Valentine, I felt my head floating away from body. I looked at the door. It was behind her.

She smirked and folded her arms as if daring me to try to get past her. "So, you're my sister, kind of."

I was lost for words, simply because it was surreal to be standing across from the woman who had been the villain in every story I'd heard about her. I looked for similarities between us. We both had dark hair. Her brown eyes were a bit lighter than mine. My cheekbones were higher and my lips poutier, and her lips were thinner yet formed into a bowtie. Julia had a softer, small-boned quality to her. I was built more like my mother and my aunt.

"What has Asher told you about me?" she asked.

All the bad stories, from extortion to her being toxically selfish, came to mind.

"I see," she said, reading my face. "That bad, huh?" She smiled, and she looked harmless.

I went to the sink to quickly wash my hands, and she walked over to stand beside me.

The water was cold, and I wished I hadn't drunk two and a half glasses of wine. My reactions were slow, and because of it, I felt vulnerable.

"Well, listen. I know we're not going to be acting as real sisters. Your mother was my father's mistress."

The words *mother* and *mistress* sounded off in my head like two consecutive gunshots. "Are you for real?" I asked, glaring at her.

"He was married to my mother, so that makes your mother his mistress."

My mouth was stuck open as I stared at her. *Does she really not comprehend what she's saying? Or is she trying to rattle me? Or is it her goal to revise history?* Maybe she needed to believe her father wasn't a man who raped little girls. He certainly wasn't my father—he was the man who raped my mother, and his violence against her had produced me.

"You know what …" I snatched a paper towel out of the holder. "Stay away from me."

I tried to walk around Julia, but she stepped in front of me.

"Move."

One of her eyes narrowed to slits. The other was glazed over. The woman looked evil. "Don't you want to know?" she asked.

"No," I said and shoved her out of my way. I could hardly believe I had done that as I took large steps toward the door, feeling the urgent need to escape.

Julia had stumbled but recovered, and she put her hand on my shoulder. "He's not a good guy, and I have proof." She sounded as if she was trying to keep her voice low.

Asher's warning repeated in my head. Julia was not to be trusted. The stark bright lights of the hallway were a welcome relief. I kept running away from her.

"Get away from me, Julia," I said as loudly as I could while thrusting my shoulder forward, trying to get her to release me. She would not let go.

Then the sight of someone else made me stop in my tracks. The woman, who was less than ten feet away from me, stopped to study me as well. We had the same dark hair. The features that were missing on Julia's face were on hers.

Julia stood beside me, her face close to mine. Her spittle sprayed my face as she said something about being in possession of a video that showed how awful Asher used to treat her, though I would have to meet her at her hotel room to see it. That was the trap, of course. The more she spoke, the farther away she sounded. Then Asher appeared behind her, and Julia finally shut her mouth.

It took a moment to see that the woman had a hand over her heart, and she looked petrified. "I heard you screaming," she said, watching Julia curiously.

Before I could respond, Asher said loudly, "Julia, follow me." His eyes stayed on mine as he walked past me.

"Who is she?" Julia asked, her curious gaze bouncing between Mary and me.

"Julia, either come with me, or I'll have security escort you out."

I could feel Julia's eyes on me, but I didn't move a muscle.

"Who is she, though?"

"Now!" Asher bellowed.

After a moment, Julia stepped away from me. I

listened to them walking away from me and was mildly worried about her being all alone with Asher. He could be trusted. She could not.

But I was in a moment that I'd thought I would never experience again. I looked into the eyes of my mother—the woman who had abandoned me. My heart wanted to combust. My eyes filled with tears. All the feelings I'd thought I had lost concerning her came rushing back through me with the velocity of Niagara Falls. It took all the strength I could muster to stay standing and not break down crying. I pulled my shoulders back. *Has she always been so beautiful?* I took a steadying breath. But first, I checked over my shoulder. I could no longer see or hear Asher and Julia. I was on my own. I had no option but to make my approach.

Twenty-Two

PENINA ROSS

Silently, with my eyes pinned to the linoleum, barely able to feel my feet hit the floor, I followed her to the lobby and out the front entrance of the building. We were lucky enough to find an unoccupied iron bench along the sidewalk. It was a Sunday afternoon. People liked to do whatever they could to avoid a hospital at that time of day. Although the weekend wasn't over, patients would start rolling in by nightfall. I thought about that as I sat down and she sat beside me, her arms folded against her chest. I wondered if she had smelled like gardenias back when I was a kid too. I didn't think so. We almost always carried the scent of dirty house and mildewed clothes.

Finally, I faced her. Mary, or Elizabeth, was already looking at me.

"What was going on back there?" she asked.

My lips parted. I considered answering but wondered if she truly deserved an answer. What had been going on back there was complex and messy and deserved an explanation she was no longer privy to.

"What are you doing here?" I asked.

Her eyes darted around my face as if she was taking in every pore and line. "I, um. Christine, um …" She closed her eyes. It was as if I'd asked her to solve a difficult math equation, but no, my question had been easy enough. "Asher Blackstone came to my door yesterday evening. Then I watched *Red Report*." She paused and looked at me as if that was supposed to ring a bell.

I shook my head. "I don't know what that is." I was running out of patience as well.

Was her skin always like porcelain?

"It's a show that gossips about famous people. And"—her eyes expanded—"Asher Blackstone is a famous person. They showed him fighting a football player at the airport, and you were with him. On top of that, Britta, one of the mothers at my son's school, said something about Greg Carroll being in our neighborhood yesterday. He was supposedly with a drunk girl. So I put it all together. It was you, wasn't it?"

A lot went through my mind. I wanted to know if that was what it took to get her to come see me—a report about a billionaire and a football player fighting. *Does she want money? Did she see an opportunity to leave her boring husband and her two bratty kids to hang with her first daughter and get a taste of the good life?*

"Okay, so you put it all together. Now what?" I asked sharply.

"Did you come to see me?"

The tears rolled, and that meant I couldn't hide behind a tough exterior. The fact that she was there and said what she had said broke my heart even more. "I did. I wanted to see you, just get a look at you, but here you are. I see you. Now you can go." I quickly stood.

"Penina."

I froze, closing my eyes. She spoke my name as if it were her own. That made my heart break even more. My name was hers because she had given it to me.

"I'm sorry. I'm here because I owe you a look at me. If that was all you wanted, I owed you that. But—"

Feet, walk away.

They wouldn't move. My neck stayed bent, eyes closed.

I turned to look at her.

"I would like to explain. Please let me explain." She looked so vulnerable and raw as she smoothed her hand over the part of the bench that I had abandoned. "Please, sit back down, please."

I folded my arms across my chest, hugging myself tightly as I carefully sat on the edge of the bench. I didn't want to be close to her. It still felt as if she were an apparition. *Can I touch her?* I hadn't touched her. Maybe I didn't want to.

"I knew you had become a surgeon. You've been a resident here at Unity Medical Center for seven years. I know your address. The people here call it the boarding hold. I've seen you at Bellies, where they have the bourbon wings, after shifts that are really hard. You have a good friend, a beautiful Indian lady with a sultry English accent. She's like a sister to you. I'm telling you all this because I've never stopped watching you. But, Penina, I can never be me again. She's gone. She's dead. And I don't want to resurrect her."

Tears streamed down my face. The fact that my mom knew all that about me suddenly made me feel loved and not as alone in the world as I'd thought I was. Finally, I could see that she was crying too.

"I hope you will one day forgive me and understand me."

I sniffed, and she opened her purse and pulled two tissues out of a plastic package and handed them to me. I hesitated. It felt like déjà vu. I was six, sitting on a bench at some desert park in Victorville, California. I felt scared and anxious. At any moment, our world could've crumbled down. I wasn't safe. I'd never felt safe, not until I met Asher. I closed my eyes and let those childhood anxieties flow out of my body then took her tissue.

"Thanks," I said then blew my nose and wiped my face.

She gave me an extra one. I used it. It wasn't until I was finished that I noticed how she was watching me.

"I love you. Always have, always will," she whispered then blew into her own tissue.

I couldn't say it back, even though it was the same for me. But I hated that I loved her. I didn't want to hate her, though. I wanted to feel nothing for her.

"You know about the man who …" She whispered.

Then it occurred to me that my mom didn't know that Julia was that man's daughter and my sister. I glanced at the exit, praying that Julia didn't walk out of the hospital.

"Yes," I said finally.

"What I went through was hell on earth. But when I looked at you, I didn't see him. I know he's in prison for what he did to me and for murdering those people at the ranch and other crimes. He's where he deserves to be. But that's not enough, Penina."

I held up a hand to silence her. "Elizbeth," I said, choosing to respect the choices she made and refer to her by her new name. "Please stop explaining. You don't have to. I'm not a little girl anymore. I'm a professional woman who's met all sorts of people in many situations in my lifetime. I've studied the brain as well. I know what we're capable of, how we can adapt, and why sometimes …" I shook my head. I was trying to convince her that I wasn't going to throw tomatoes at her or hate her forever.

"Listen, when I met Asher Blackstone, he was calling himself Jake Sparrow." I barked a laugh at the irony that my mother and my boyfriend had both chosen to assume new identities. "I'm just saying that I'm not judging you. That's all. I understand why you did what you did."

"You were a good child, though. It wasn't you. It was me. You didn't deserve me, the way I was then."

I wanted her to stop talking but also wanted to hear more. "Like I said, you don't have to explain."

She closed her eyes and shook her hands as she said, "I want to say this. I have to." Then she breathed in and out slowly through her nostrils.

I pressed my lips together and nodded, giving her the space and grace to get whatever she wanted off her chest.

"My two children are a lot more work than you were. You were such a good baby and a good little girl." Her gaze caressed my face. "You did everything I ever asked without question. No back talk. No whining. My husband is fine. I couldn't expect Prince Charming from a man who doesn't know or want to know who I really am. I imagine he has his secrets too. But …" She closed her eyes and aimed her face toward the sun.

I held my tongue. My insides wanted to burst into flames. *Did she not know why I was such a good little girl?* I was scared all the time. I'd had to be good because I knew she wanted to leave me. Every waking moment, I knew. So I had to be obedient so that she wouldn't go, even though she eventually did what I'd been afraid of.

I stared at her face, thinking maybe if I looked hard enough, I could transfer some of my thoughts to her and she would understand. I didn't want to tell her what I was thinking, perhaps because in the end—and it was the end as far she and I were concerned—the truth didn't matter. We would be two generations of estranged Rosses. Looking at her face, I realized she wasn't there seeking to get back into my life. She was making peace with leaving me. I vowed never to make the same mistake with my children.

"No more," I said with a sigh and rose to my feet. "I have to get back inside."

Even though I didn't. I had no meetings or HR paperwork to sign, not that day, at least. I'd been told all of that as part of my surprise farewell party, which had ended before I went to the ladies' room. But I had reached my limit. Being near Elizabeth Thomas made me feel as if I was being smothered.

I frowned at her wide-eyed gaze.

"I understand," she whispered.

319

She had a hint of uncertainty in her tone, but I didn't care. Turning my back on her, I said, "Have a good life."

At first, I walked briskly, then I shuffled my feet. I would've run from her but didn't want to rouse anyone's concern. But ultimately, I did, and I gasped for air and pulled at the top of my silky camisole. My skin was hot and my head heavy. Too many people asked if I was okay, and too many hands touched me. I recognized all the faces, but their names escaped me. *Mary Ross. Elizabeth Thomas.* The names kept repeating in my head. My body was rigid as I squeezed my balled fist against my collarbone and pressed my arms against my breasts. *Stop touching me.* I wanted to say it, but those words wouldn't come out.

Finally, all the bodies around me began to recede. Dr. Pittman told them all to give me air because I was having a panic attack.

"Penina!" Asher's voice rose above the rest of the chatter.

So desperately, I searched for him through my blurry vision. Then two strong arms swooped me off the hard floor as if I were feather light. Asher's scent filled my senses. With my face buried in the crook of his neck, I clung to him, relishing the warmth of his skin as he took swift steps. Soon the outside air bathed me. I gasped as if I'd finally made it to the surface of the ocean to release the breaths that had been trapped in my lungs.

ASHER CLIMBED INTO THE BACK SEAT OF HIS CAR with me. Kirk drove us back to the Four Seasons. I was more exhausted than when I worked a night call and was summonsed less than twelve hours later to perform a six-hour surgery. I was broken, shaking, and clinging to Asher like a scared kitten.

He kept rubbing my shoulder and kissing my forehead. I was embarrassed to be so weak in his presence, but I couldn't seem to pull myself out of my emotional state. It wanted to get worse, not better—and I was ready to recover already.

"Asher," I said, my voice trembling.

"It's all right, babe." He kissed me on the forehead again.

"No, I'm fine." I shifted to sit up on my own, willing myself to battle the grief.

He cautiously let go of me. "You can just rest, Penina. You were hit with a lot at once. I should've stayed closer to you."

I wanted to smile at him, just to prove that I was fine, but the corners of my mouth were too heavy to lift.

Falling back against the seat, I sighed as my eyes flitted closed. "You couldn't have prevented my mom showing up or Julia trapping me in the ladies' room." I massaged my temples. "What a crazy two days I've had." Actually, the craziness had been more than two days. It had all started about a month ago when Rich and Courtney strolled into Bellies to inform me that they were a couple. Shortly thereafter, I ran into Jake Sparrow.

"Is this how it's supposed to feel?"

He rubbed my thigh comfortingly. "How what is supposed to feel?"

"Deep, meaningful change."

"Hmm. How does it feel?"

"Like I'm being run over by a freight—"

Suddenly, I knew what I needed—the cure.

"What is it, babe?" Asher asked.

I stopped massaging my temples. My eyelids were lighter as I looked at him. "There's somewhere I need to go."

Twenty-Three

PENINA ROSS

We walked into Bellies, and I felt like I was home again. The eatery was crowded for a Sunday afternoon, but just as if fate were welcoming me back to the place where it all started, a couple got up from the bar, and the two seats where Rich and Courtney had ambushed me opened up. Asher also saw the vacancies and took my hand. We made a beeline to them.

My smile felt as luminous as the moon when my butt hit the cushion, and so was his.

"Why are you so happy all of a sudden?" he asked, still grinning.

"Because you're here with me, and I've come full circle."

I could see by the slight way that his eyes narrowed that he had no idea what I was talking about. Heck, he probably thought I had gone crazy. I didn't want him to think that, so I guided my lips toward his and initiated a gentle kiss.

Yes, his mouth tasted delicious. Yes, his tongue felt good brushing against mine. Yes, my head floated away from my body. Then I guided my mouth next to his ear so he could hear me above the ambient noise.

"I left this place the morning I ran into you in front of my building, smoking a cigarette." I kissed his cheek. "And now I'm in love with you."

Asher captured my face in his hands and once again pressed his lips against mine.

"I love you, too, babe. And about your mother—"

I pressed a finger on his lips. "She's not my mother, not anymore—and I don't ever want to talk about her."

We stared into each other's eyes. He seemed conflicted. I was not.

"Pen? Are you back?"

I leaned to the side to see around Asher. It was Corey, a cool blond bartender with shaggy hair.

Asher twisted his body around to get a look at him.

"Yes, I'm back," I sang as I leaned forward, putting one hand on Asher's solid thigh and holding up two fingers with the other. "Can I have two orders of bourbon wings with hot buttery biscuits for me and my man here?"

Corey's eyes shifted to Asher as though he'd just noticed he was sitting next to me.

"Oh, okay. Got it. Sparkling water with lemon?" he asked.

"For both of us," I said.

Corey looked at Asher just to confirm that it was okay to go with my order. I knew it was fine. I'd learned a lot about Asher-Jake during our time together. One thing was that he wouldn't drink alcohol if I wasn't having any, unless something was vexing him. That was how I'd instinctively known he recognized the woman on the night of the masquerade party—he had ordered scotch on the rocks.

"Bourbon wings, huh?" he asked.

"Rich doctors don't eat bourbon wings?" I asked.

He sniffed, regarding me carefully. "What's

wrong with you? Why the big change all of a sudden?"

I inhaled deeply then let it go. "Because there's nothing I can do about Elizabeth or Julia."

"You don't have to worry about Julia," he said in a rush. "She's been handled."

"What did you do to her?" I asked.

He told me that he didn't want Julia anywhere near Mary Ross, so he'd escorted her back to her office and told her to get to work. She seemed surprised she wasn't fired, so without a second word, she sat at her desk, turned on her computer, and started working.

"I had to thwart her expectations," he said.

Smiling a little, I asked, "Thwart them?"

He sniffed. "Exactly. If I had kept fighting with Julia, then she would've fought too."

"Ah," I said, nodding. "After I pushed her, she latched on to me like a gnat."

"You pushed her?"

My shoulders hunched. "She tried to block me, so I had to get physical." I shook my head, banishing the memory of our little altercation. "She's crazy."

"Good for you, babe. I bet she thought she could push you around."

I smirked. "Did you think she could push me around?"

Asher's lips found mine, and we kissed tenderly. "You're a delicate flower who's tough as nails."

I chuckled against his mouth. "You thought she would push me around."

Asher laughed.

"I'm badass, you know?"

"Who's badass?" a woman with a sultry English accent asked.

I whipped my head around to see Zara.

"Hey, KitKat," she said, initiating a hug.

"Love you, Reece's Pieces," I said as we embraced.

EVERYTHING AFTER THAT HAPPENED SO appropriately and so fast. Zara was with Sarah, who probably hadn't seen Asher since the night of the fire, and just as she had then, she eye-mugged him from the moment she saw him. Then Asher went to get Kirk, and he joined us as at a bigger table. We talked about everything from politics, which started with Zara asking Asher about his brother, who ran for Senate against his wife's mother, to some of the new articles in *Neuro Journal Today*. It surprised me that Zara still read it. I took it as a good sign.

Then Asher's twin sister called, heard all the noise, and asked if she could join us. By the time she showed up, a typical New Orleans street band had set up. From the first song they played, Asher had taken my hand, cleared some room, and held me against him, and we danced, kissed, and gazed into each other's eyes.

Then Bryn Blackstone, tall, beautiful, blond, and a dead ringer for Asher, walked into the restaurant with another beautiful woman and a man, who was as just as good-looking as Asher. Cell phone cameras flashed. People got excited. Everyone knew Jasper Walker Blackstone and his wife, Holly Henderson Blackstone. Zara and Holly seemed to get along, as they talked endlessly about current events. As Asher had once said, Bryn and I had more in common. Asher was a favorite topic of ours. He listened with a sheepish grin as his sister and I compared notes. I said I loved the way he folded my clothes when I tossed them here and there.

"Oh, he's a neat freak," Bryn said. "Has he cooked for you yet?"

I nodded, rubbing his thigh. "Scallops."

She smiled at him approvingly. "So, what are you two going to do for Pen's sabbatical?" Bryn had heard Zara call me Pen and decided she would rather refer to me by the informal version of my name, since she was triple-sure I would be around the family for a long time.

Asher flicked his eyebrows up twice. And on cue, Bryn and I rolled our eyes at the same time then chuckled about it.

"Besides that, Ash," she said.

Asher scratched the back of his neck. "I want to take her somewhere. A place she's never been."

Bryn's eyes lit up. "Good idea. And I have some suggestions."

Then Bryn, Asher, and I talked about all the places we could go and where we could stay until Zara held out her hand and asked me to cut a rug with her before she left.

And we did.

And we danced.

And we laughed.

And we were happy.

Twenty-Four

PENINA ROSS

That was the night my life began anew. After Asher and I made it back to the penthouse, we made love until Monday afternoon—no sleep, just kissing, touching, and sex. He skipped the big staff meeting. He said that Si would handle it. Julia had already spread the rumor that Asher and his brothers purchased the hospital. The report from the chief was that no one was bitter about it. Everyone had bought the story that Asher was pretending to be Jake Sparrow to assess whether he would purchase the hospital. Their sentiments were aided by the fact that EBHI would be part of the hospital's infrastructure, and fifty percent more nurses, doctors, and surgeons would be hired within the next six months.

It was the last week of September. Asher and I had been traveling together for nearly three months, and the next week, we were due back at the hospital. Our journey had started in New Zealand, where we frolicked in blue pools, hiked over glaciers, searched for waterfalls, and slept under the night skies.

Next, we flew to Norway, where we cruised riverways aboard private superyachts, took long drives through twisty grassy mountains, and gazed over tall cliffs to wonder at the most beautiful landscapes of rocks, grass, and zigzagging streams below.

There was no rhyme or reason for deciding where we chose to go. Asher and I discovered we both had a hankering for marveling at and wallowing in the most beautiful aspects of nature. We both loved connecting with people, too, so we took Bryn's advice and participated in some of the local food-and-wine festivals in small communities from Portugal to Spain to France to Italy then up to Ireland. We saw a lot of people who, as Bryn had said, didn't recognize Asher Blackstone. It also helped that Asher was multilingual, which surprised the heck out of me. He spoke Spanish, Italian, German, and Portuguese.

We gave ourselves two days in Japan's Yoshino-Kumano National Park, where we rowed our boat among clusters of rock formations and walked the Kumano Kodo trail to visit an ancient shrine. All the trails felt surreal, dwarfed by tall trees with mossy barks. With all the illustrious sights we'd seen and ancient ground we had walked, the absolute best part of our travels had been gazing into each other's eyes over candlelit dinners and cooling our bodies in semi-comfortable beds after making love as Asher used his hands to explain the mineral components of the volcanic soil we'd walked across. He knew a lot about land formations and land use. Whenever we encountered local farmers, he would engage them in long conversations about their crops, even lending them tips at times but mostly reeling with excitement when he learned something new from them. I was in awe of how smart he was, and that endeared him to me even more.

After leaving Japan, we decided it was time for a change of pace, especially since our vacation would soon be over and we didn't want to return to work exhausted from our time off. We opted to explore the Andaman Sea on a superyacht, replacing hiking with snorkeling and swimming in blue lagoons. We dined on five-star meals whipped up by a private chef and made love in a comfortable bed.

Unlike with Rich, Asher and I never ran out of things to talk about. Over breakfast, we discussed the Expansive Brain Health Institute, which was something we were very excited about. Being surgeons, we showed each other techniques, practicing on melons. We discussed Elizabeth Thomas. I was finally able to feel deep inside what I'd said to Asher. I told him that at the moment—and I could only live in the here and now—she was like a whisper that had been carried away by the wind, although my nostrils tightened and tears pooled in my eyes if I thought about her too long.

"That's okay, Penina. You love her. Honor that and let it be."

I beamed at him so brightly that perfect warmth spread across my face. "I will. Thank you."

Then his expression mirrored mine.

Traveling together had showed us how kind and patient we were with each other. Perhaps it was because we were both brain surgeons that we knew how to listen to each other and those around us. That was why, during our last stop in another superyacht on the Arctic Ocean, I knew without a doubt I was made for him and him for me. We both had been derived from turmoil and ugliness. He had met his mother, and she was still alive, but before, he'd been too angry with his father and ashamed of what happened to her to build any sort of relationship with her. Bryn was in a relationship with their mom, though. He had another sister, and he felt the same way about her too. He asked if I could help him, if I would be his strength as we sat with the two of them, sharing a meal and getting to know them better.

I squeezed his hands and said, "Of course, my love. Anything you want."

Yes, at some point during our travels, I began to refer to Asher as my love. *He is my love.*

It was nine p.m. Asher had gone to the kitchen to retrieve a bottle of champagne. I was inside the heated glass dome on top of the vessel, naked on the king-sized bed and under a white faux-fur blanket. Not a single cloud blocked the light-green beams and sprays of green light streaking through the atmosphere like clusters of haunting spirits. The colors became more vivid through the telescope glasses we wore to view the phenomenon. Bryn had been right. The aurora borealis, also known as the northern lights, was the most wonderful spectacle I'd had the privilege to lay eyes on.

I kept thinking about Bryn, recalling the last time I'd seen her and Asher's family, or at least the people he'd grown up with. It had been two days after our fun night at Bellies. Asher and I had arrived at the mansion at seven p.m. He rang the doorbell three times before opening the door. My dormmate, Nat, used to do the same thing whenever we arrived at her family's house in Baton Rouge for the holiday. The fact that Asher's family had the same habit made me feel aglow inside. I was in love with a man who had his own version of Rich's family, and he was someone I could trust and count on.

After the ringing ended, an excited little girl came to the door. "Daddy!" She spoke gibberish until she said, "Ash here!"

Asher and I raised our eyebrows at each other.

The little girl had long, wavy brown hair and was wearing cut-off denim pedal pushers and a blue-and-white-striped shirt. She rushed Asher and wrapped herself around his leg. "You're my uncle!"

Her name was Jane, and she was Jasper's daughter. Asher had been nervous about meeting her for the first time. But she was so excited to meet him. It was as though, for her, a new uncle was like a new toy for her birthday.

My shoulders shook when I laughed. I was just so tickled. Jane was the cutest little thing I'd ever seen. The only reason she could already know Asher and love him even though she'd never seen him was because she felt loved and secure. I could never have been that way at her age, and perhaps that was why tears filled my eyes as I laughed.

And after the shock passed, Asher hoisted her off the ground, and tickling her little tummy, he said, "Yes, I am your uncle. And you must be Jane, my cute-as-a-button niece."

"I'm Jane," she sang, nudging herself in the chest. Next, she pointed at me. "And you're Pen!"

My eyes sparkled when I said, "Yes, I am!"

Asher and I flexed our eyebrows at each other as she hugged him around the neck. Then she asked to be put down so that she could take us to the den where her mom, dad, aunt Bryn, Jada, and uncle Spencer were waiting for us.

After we all shook hands and hugged, we moseyed into the patio dining room for dinner. I had never been a fan of lobster until I ate Chef Bart's chili lemon lobster over a bed of avocado with fresh mint and lime shrimp ceviche. We were also served antipasto salad with European cheeses and freshly baked breads. I was asked the standard questions—where I was from and why I'd chosen to become a neurosurgeon. But that was all. The Blackstones didn't practice prying.

Jasper's wife, Holly, seemed to be the one who absorbed every small detail about me. She could see how nervous I was and how out of place I felt as the brothers talked about their plans for the hospital.

"Now, Dr. Ross," Jasper said, leaning forward.

Holly winked at me. "It's Pen, honey."

"Right, sorry, Pen. Do you envision yourself playing an administrative role in the hospital?" He sounded as if he were giving me a job interview.

I turned to Asher, who appeared just as shocked by Jasper's question as I was.

"Um, that'll be a no," I said. "I'm a surgeon." I raised a finger pointedly. "Research, though, yes!"

His hard expression eased into a smile as he nodded. "Okay … I see."

"Why do you ask?" I asked.

"If or when you become a Blackstone, you'll have the option."

I leaned back against my seat. Goodness, he certainly wasn't one to finesse things. He went straight to the finish line.

"Jas, come on," Asher said, pulling at his collar while squirming.

"What?" he asked, throwing his hands up as if he didn't get it.

"But isn't this great?" Bryn asked, garnering everyone's attention. "Remember the last time all four of us and Holly had dinner together?"

Spencer grunted. "At the mansion."

"Bryn, I heard you had it demolished, and now they're rebuilding," Holly said.

Bryn smiled from ear to ear. "It's almost finished. We have to spend Christmas there, all of us." She tilted her head, eyeing each and every one of her brothers individually. "And I mean all of us."

"I'm in," Spencer said.

"Yes, we'll be there," Jasper said.

Asher interlaced his fingers with mine under the table. "So will we."

"Aha," Jada, Spencer's wife, said. "Then you guys are going to be married. Mark my words."

"Yeah," Spencer said, nodding. "They're tying the knot. Absolutely."

"I would like that," Jasper said. "I like you, Dr. Ross."

Holly chuckled as she rubbed her husband's back. "He just likes saying Dr. Ross."

"Dr. Ross!" Jane repeated excitedly, and we all laughed.

Throughout the rest of dinner, Bryn led the family in an exercise in which they only shared good memories from the past while Jane sat on her lap. Jasper recounted the time Spencer got the idea to do a backflip off a private yacht while it was in motion. He would've been lost in the middle of the South Pacific if Jasper hadn't gotten to the captain in time and had him retrace their path. The current had carried him five miles off course. They finally found him before nightfall.

"Father was never told about that?" Asher asked.

"No," Jasper said. "He didn't need to know."

"How old were you then?" Jada asked, looking at Spencer.

"Thirteen."

"Then, Jasper, you were only fifteen," Jada said. "You never cease to amaze me."

Jasper shrugged. "I did what needed to be done, that's all."

They talked about cheerier memories like swimming in the sound, which their property curved around. They had to admit that they were struggling to pinpoint the good times.

"Well, we'll make happy memories now, starting with tonight," Bryn said.

"Actually, Sunday night was a blast," Holly added.

We all agreed.

After dessert, we sat under the stars, and I listened as they all talked about their plans to connect with one another. Holly would be helping Jada with a fundraiser for the Spencer and Jada Blackstone Foundation. Bryn was going to work with the foundation to help set up shelters for people who had fallen victim to sex trafficking in the US. They discussed a preventative aspect of targeting the issue of illegal trafficking, hoping to figure out how to help people before they ended up in the clutches of traffickers. Then the conversation turned to a bakery in Santa Barbara, and it wasn't until Holly gave Jada tips on being pregnant that I noticed she was indeed with child.

All in all, the night was perfect—so perfect that when Asher and I made it back to the penthouse, I found my shoebox and the letter my mom used to make me keep. I'd had two glasses of the most delicious red wine that night, so as we sat on the balcony, spectators of a summer moon and lively riverboats, I peeled open the seal of the letter. I couldn't read it, though, so I handed it to Asher, who read it for me.

I closed my eyes as I listened to him say, "If you're reading this, then it means I'm not coming back. The girl's name is Penina Ross, and she is my daughter. I have tried to love her as a mother should, but I can't. She's better off without me, and I'm better off without her. Please contact her aunt, Christine Louise Ross, and not my parents. My parents are the reason I cannot love as I should. They will destroy her like they did me. Call Christine and only Christine." Then she gave my aunt's address and phone number.

Asher and I stared at each other. I was choked up, but the last three days had been too happy for me to cry.

"Well, there I have it," I whispered.

He smiled and held out his hand. "Let's go to bed."

We slept that night because I had started my period. But three days later, we got on an airplane to our first vacation destination, and unfortunately, we were close to the end of our wonderful romp around the world.

"What are you smiling about?" Asher asked.

I took off my scope glasses that made me feel as

if I could touch the aurora borealis and beamed at him. He was standing in the doorway, wearing pajama bottoms and a thick black turtleneck sweater and holding something.

"Ha!" I gasped, slapping my hands over my mouth.

Asher dropped down to one knee. "My beautiful Penina. Would you do me the honor of walking through this world with me from now until forever?"

There was only one answer I could give him. My hands shook, and tears rolled freely when I said that one fated word.

Epilogue

PENINA ROSS

"Penina?" Asher's voice gusted through my mind like leaves rustling in the wind.

My eyes flickered open as I eased into full consciousness.

"Babe, we're here," he whispered.

Hearing the emotion coloring his tone, I reached over to massage his solid bicep. Asher had been nervous about arriving at his childhood home. Bryn had completed final renovations in February of that year. It would be the first time he would lay eyes on the gory mansion.

Even though Bryn had become one of my closest friends, I'd never seen the mansion, either. I wanted to experience it with Asher, and at that very moment, the day before our wedding. Most of our guests would be staying in town at an inn owned by the Blackstones. However, all of our family members would have rooms at the mansion. For me, that included Aunt Christine, who was bringing a date, and Zara, who was like a sister to me. Kirk, who was her boyfriend, would be staying with us well.

All of Asher's siblings and their partners would be in attendance. Beth McConnell, Asher's biological mother, would also be there. We were both excited about that. In April, he and I tore ourselves from our work at the hospital and flew out to California to see her. Leading up to our visit, Bryn had sent him plenty of pictures of his mother. He had told me her appearance was starkly different than he remembered. She'd put on a healthy amount of weight, when before, her skin hugged her bones. Also, the scant number of teeth she had left were rotted. But in the photos, she flashed smiles with a full set of perfectly straight and pearly-white teeth. I had finally read the biography, *The Dark Blackstones*, and from it, I learned how Asher and his siblings came to know of Beth's existence. One night before our trip, after we had made love, he confessed that as Jake Sparrow, he had wiped Beth out of his memory. From the moment he ever laid eyes on her, he wished he'd never met her. The fact that his father was a pedophile, and his mother, a former prostitute and drug addict, was too much to bear. Bryn was the one who stuck with Beth, getting her the help needed. It had taken four stints in rehab before Beth could wrap her mind around the fact that she was not trash. She was a human being worthy of love, respect, and happiness.

We had taken Beth to brunch at Tutto Pao, an Italian and Chinese fusion restaurant in Bel Air, which had breathtaking views of the westside. During the car ride to the restaurant, she and I mostly talked about my work as a surgeon. It was as if she was afraid to say anything to Asher as if the wrong words would send him away from her forever.

But at some point, I mentioned a procedure that Asher and I were working on perfecting, and I was thankful he was a chemist because he was able to use mathematics to get us past barriers. That was when Beth mentioned one of her brothers was also a mathematician.

"Brothers? I have uncles?" Asher asked.

She smiled. "Yes. They're younger than me. They didn't know I existed until Caroline, my therapist, reached out to them."

And from that moment on, Asher and Beth couldn't stop talking to each other. Over dinner, she told us everything—the bad, the worse, and the ultra-ugly. But she shared the good too, which occurred the moment Bryn walked into her life and changed it forever.

I would always remember every aspect of what happened next. Night had fallen, and the lukewarm air carried the scent of the Pacific Ocean. We'd eaten dinner and were having dessert when Asher said, "I'm sorry, Beth..." He cleared his throat. "Mom. I'm sorry I wasn't there for you like Bryn was. But that's Bryn; we can always rely on her in that way. But I'm here for you." He took my hand in his and looked me in the eyes. "We both are." He nodded.

I nodded back.

As it was that night at Tutto Pao, it was hard to rip my eyes away from Asher's face then, and put them on the famed mansion that had launched Bryn's new career as an interior designer. His lips were parted as the sight rendered him speechless. Gawking at his beautiful profile was like being lost in the allure of the form and fitness of Michelangelo's *David*.

Then he turned to me, eyes glistening, smile perfect. "Wow, I didn't expect that."

I moved my lips towards his and closed my eyes as we engaged in a delicate but rousing kiss. Our persistent tongues wanted to continue brushing and tasting each other, but it was now time to see what had made the man that loved so emotional.

JULIA VALENTINE

The Day After The Wedding

I'd been waiting for The Daily Chronicle to post captures of Asher's wedding. There he was, holding her hand—Penina Ross. My sister by blood only. Her dress was white, of course. But how tacky—a plunging neckline. If I were marrying a Blackstone, my dress would've had a boatneck or a Queen Anne neckline. They were all in attendance— Jasper, Spencer, Bryn, and even Gina had been invited.

I scream my head off as I shot to my feet and turned my back on the computer screen.

Closing my eyes, I filled my lungs with air. I thought about the day I followed Penina into the restroom at the hospital. My intention was not to set her off that way.

What was my intention then?

I just wanted to talk to her. I wanted to know if Asher truly loved her. But I should've kept my distance.

My eyes quickly open as I touch my throat. A sweetheart neckline. Yes, that was it. My dress would've had a sweetheart neckline.

Then I remembered the Monday morning when Jasper threatened to ruin me forever. I was actually ecstatic about getting to work on the press release touting the new sports medicine wing of the hospital. I liked my job. I was good at it. But I knew I made a bonafide enemy out of the Blackstones when I threatened Asher with exposing Bryn's drug dealing. *Stupid move.* I wouldn't have told anyone. And I wished that on Monday morning when one of the Blackstones showed up to threaten and fire me, it wasn't Jasper. He was the one man I hadn't wanted to face.

Imposing and intimidating, Jasper Blackstone's frame filled the doorway.

"Stephanie, leave us," he said without looking at her.

Stephanie, who wasn't one to be pushed around, let her survival instincts guide her.

"Of course, Mr. Blackstone," she muttered. Then, without question, she got up from her desk, her high heels pitter-pattering out the door.

My breathing went shallow, my skin warmed, and my head felt as if it detached from my body. Jasper smelled good and looked sexy in a pair of heather gray slacks and a white crisp button-down shirt. But I couldn't let his appearance fool me. He was an avenging angel, sentencing me to destitution.

"What can I do for you?" I mustered enough courage to ask.

He stared at me with an unreadable expression. I heard my heart beating and felt it too. He still hadn't said anything. Jasper wanted me to do exactly what I was doing—stand before him, trembling like a leaf in the wind.

"We were once on good terms, weren't we?" he asked.

I swallowed the lump in my throat, knowing that I was prey, and he was the predator, toying with his kill.

"I wanted you to be the least of my worries, Julia. But now you're the cause of what's worrying me the most. It wouldn't take more than an hour to make that nagging feeling go away. Do you understand me?" One of his eyes had narrowed slightly. He was angry. I couldn't grab his cock or unbutton my blouse and offer him my breasts. None of that worked on Jasper Blackstone—never had, never would.

I... I didn't know what to say. I wanted to plead for mercy and accuse him of ruining my family. I no longer had any friends. Everyone abandoned me after hearing what my father had done to those women. And then there were the videos. I couldn't wipe them out of my memory, even though I have tried. *I know he committed those crimes. But I can never admit. If I did, I would lose everything.*

"You were supposed to marry me, take care of me. That was the deal between our fathers," I said.

He glanced over his shoulder. The door was still ajar, and knowing Jasper, he hadn't wanted anyone to hear what I had just said.

"But that wasn't our deal. I never agreed to

marry you. However, you've threatened Asher and Bryn. You've accosted Dr. Ross. And, you've extorted some of my former employees."

My lips parted. Once again, I was on the verge of accusing the Blackstones of abandoning the Valentines. But Bryn was still close to Carter, my brother. He wouldn't even take my calls or agree to meet me. At that moment, for some strange reason, I remembered the last words I spoke to Carter. I had put together a string of insults my father used to call him. I was mean, unloving. *I loved my brother. Didn't I?*

But the look in Jasper's eyes said he didn't give a damn about my woes. I felt trapped. It was as if I were living the final moments before the blade of the guillotine sliced through my neck.

Dispensing judgment, he turned his back on me. "I'll be in touch."

"Wait," I called, realizing it was time to fight for the little I had left.

Thankfully, Jasper stopped in his tracks. "Make it good." His back was still turned.

"I did it. Everything you said, I did it." My confession made me want to barf.

Never admit defeat, I heard my father say in my head.

"I know that already."

Anxiously, I rubbed my palms together. "I don't know why I do what I do. Survival, maybe. But, I will leave your family, Dr. Ross, everyone alone. If you just don't hurt me." I inhaled deeply, and my throat trembled as I released the air and whispered, "Please."

I was weak and a mess. But my fate was in his hands. Come tomorrow, I could be poor, or I could still be rich. The choice was his.

Still, with his back facing me, he stood very still. "You're fired, Julia. Leave the hospital and the city."

Then he walked away.

I opened my eyes, and tears welled up inside them. That was last year. Jasper had chosen not to bankrupt me. And I kept my promise; I backed off from the Blackstones. But what had I gotten in return? My sister, who was the result of my father's sins, was a Blackstone, and I was not.

But one thing's for certain. I sniffed and wiped my tears. I pulled my shoulders back, standing tall. And then, I smiled. *Because this is true indeed—one day, like a Phoenix out of the ashes, I will rise again.*

Next comes Destined, the FINAL book of The
Blackstone Brothers featuring the only sister
—Bryn.

———————

If You haven't read the earlier books of this series, then
start with INTRIGUED.

Printed in Great Britain
by Amazon

23378206R00198